Dedications

This book is dedicated to anyone who buys it.

No, seriously. I need the cash.

Also: Casey Morell for proofreading, the thousands of blog visitors I get each month for keeping this idea buoyant, and the University of York for supplying me with a course that gives me a lot of free time.

Also by Christopher J. Fraser

The Chewy Cerebrum and Other Stories (with Joseph O'Brien)

TALES FROM THE END

a compilation

Written by

Christopher J. Fraser

Published by Hiatus Press

www.chrisjfraser.com

First published 2009
1

Typeset in Constantia and Arial by Christopher Fraser.

Made and printed in the UK by Lulu Self-Publishing plc

ISBN 978-0-9561519-2-6

Tales From The End

A compilation

Stories, streams of consciousness and abstract concepts from the years 2008, 2009 and 2010

CONTENTS

Part One - Genesis

Part Two – Exodus

Part Three – Revelations

Blind

I'm walking down the street, walking my dog, when my eyes suddenly disappear from their sockets.

Of course, at first I think I've gone blind, but it's when I try and blink that I realise that my eyes have actually gone. Where before there were two slimy, globular structures with a tiny hole through the centre through which something in my head would work out the world around me, now there's just two dry holes.

I am the Eyeless Man.

I wonder about becoming an enigmatic presence. I can get used to being blind, and people are perverse enough to want to see a living, breathing freak. I raise my hand up to my face. I can't feel any blood, or seeping tissue. It seems like the scars my eyes' disappearance have left are unnoticeable.

When I hear the screaming, I firstly think that they're screaming at me. You know, because I've got two holes in my head. It would, after all, make sense. If the eyeballs of the man on the street suddenly decide that they're bored of this dimension and want a holiday, you don't stop to tell them that Majorca's nice this time of year. You do what people seem to be doing, and scream out in surprised horror.

But it's when the screaming seems to be coming from miles away too that I begin to question myself. Surely only those nearby can see my predicament? Even the man on the other side of the street can't see this. Then I twig, thanks to the shrill screech of a woman somewhere behind me.

"AAAAAAAGH! MY EYES! MY FOOKIN' EYES!"

What a melody – like Tchaikovsky played through shitty 90s Europop, all against the backdrop of a faulty buzzsaw. Heaven.

What this does tell me, on the other hand, is that I'm not alone in my condition.

I need to make sure. I start flailing around, not yet fully possessed of a bat-like echolocation ability, and eventually my right arm comes into contact with a small child. The kid yells out as he or she goes flying onto the pavement, and I kneel by the source of the crying. I begin to trace out their face, and am suddenly thankful that people probably can't see this - any other time, and I would be locked up for battery and paedophilia. I eventually find her (it's either a she, or a boy ready to take a lifetime of bullying) young visage, and despite her physical and verbal protests, seek out her eye sockets. I take in a deep breath of air, and finally press my fingers down through the eyelids.

Nothing. Nothing at all. Utter emptiness, two vacant spaces where eyes should be. But then - ow! Something, definitely something... but what? I feel my fingers to discover the source of the pain, then do a double take - tiny teeth marks. Have our eyes grown teeth? Is that what's happened? I raise my own hands to my face - wary of what might happen - and against my reflexes I reach into the vacuous holes where my glorious eyes were once in, and scoop out a small creature. It squeals as I pinch it between my finger and thumb.

I feel around, squish the monster a little, and figure it's made out of some sort of rubbery flesh. It's screaming, or at least emitting a really high-pitched frequency. I'm getting a headache, so I throw the creature down on the floor, where it lands with a *splat*.

A year and a half down the line, the world will remember that the end started in this small town in the North of England. Everything that happens from today will sweep a localised event like this under the carpet, but this will be the first day of the chaos to come – the day when all of fifteen thousand people in a small English town lost their eyes.

Christmas

I wake up in Victorian London. This has happened before, and thankfully I was clever last time and secured lodging for a year or two. I have a habit of waking up in different eras, and as yet I have no idea how to stop it. Time travel's fun when it's planned, but when you've got no control it's just another day job. You make do.

There is a man, clad in orange robes, wearing a sandwich board, shouting and cawing on the high street. The sandwich-board reads "COME INSIDE FOR A CHRISTMAS TALE OF MYSTERY AND JOY," and the language the man speaks in is of some strange, incomprehensible tongue that slowly reveals itself to me as he beckons me closer. No-one else notices him but me. I stare at him, transfixed by the bellowing black man in his fluorescent attire. This is a bitter, Victorian winter, right in the heart of London. Dim gas lamps, shut curtains, horse-drawn carts dragged along by equine depression. Street urchins, begging for change in the shadows, ignored by the high-class ladies and gentlemen. Hardly the place for someone so bold. How everyone else seems to not notice the man escapes me; they just veer around him without looking at him twice.

I walk closer, and his words become clearer. He's shouting phrases like "roll up, roll up" and "in for a penny, in for a pound" - strange, archaic phrases to my ears, and ones that don't quite make sense out of context. I avoid the carts, and blink back the icy cold as I walk. I'm fascinated by this man. It may be a morbid fascination, but the curiosity is still there. Tears, defence against the cold, form in my eyes, disorientating me. I raise my gloved hand to my face to wipe them away, and when I draw my hand back again I realise I'm standing right in front of the man. I can't help but think: *funny, he was at least a hundred yards off before.*

He looks at me, seeing me for the first time, and his face breaks out into a beam: he has a customer.

"You want to hear a story, mister? You say yes, I'll tell you an epic tale of love, discov'ry, and excitement. One shilling." I shrug, and fumble around in my pocket for some loose change. It takes a while. You think working in a currency exchange is hard – try having valid currency for every state since the birth of civilisation.

I finally surface with a couple of coins. He takes them, then swallows me whole, and everything changes.

I'm sat in a cart, trundling down the man's gullet. There are more carts, behind and in front of me, as if I'm on some sort of mining expressway, but there's no-one but me in this tunnel. I'm on the way to the stomach, I guess. I begin to wonder what it'll be like, to be digested by this man's stomach acid. Painful, probably. But that's OK. I don't mind pain. I don't *like* it, don't get me wrong, but it doesn't bother me too much. There are probably worse things than being eaten alive by acid. Probably. I never really put that much thought into it.

What I *am* worried about is that, given I'm likely to die within the next few minutes, I can't think of any brilliant last words. I reason that this is probably due to the shock of being swallowed alive by a man only marginally taller than I am, only to discover that by contrast, his insides are cavernous. A series of events like that doesn't exactly lend the average human being to a state of quick-wittedness. If I said anything now, it would probably be a comment like "I am trundling down a man's oesophagus, which is inexplicably considerably larger than I am." This isn't a particularly inspiring sentence to end one's life with, so I stay silent. This way, my last word - "bye," to my wife (earlier this afternoon, but just as easily to the world) - has a certain understated poignancy to it.

It's almost time. I see the tunnel coming to a stop up ahead, blocked by a giant sphincter in the shape of a cat-flap. I duck, hoping that I'll at least glimpse the stomach before I plunged to my death, rather than smacking my head on the flap and suffering severe concussion.

It works, but at first I'm doubtful because what happens isn't what I expect. My eyes shut, I feel a jolt as the cart whisks round to the right and carries on, gradually picking up speed, and music penetrates my ears - some buzzing, fast-paced rendition of "Hark! The Herald Angels Sing", with an array of instruments that I don't recognise.

I carefully lift myself up from the foetal position I'm in, and peer over the side of the cart. Everything I expected - half-digested food, acres of bile and vomit - is absent, replaced with a bustling factory floor, with hordes of tiny-looking people running to and fro, carrying an assortment of different brightly-coloured packages.

The cart and rolls and spirals around the lining of the man's stomach, still getting faster and faster, with me inside hanging on for dear life. I see the world outside the cart and winces, my head sustained bend to for the most part, as if in prayer. The cart keeps going down and round, down and round.

First, I hear a dull thud, then I'm flying through the air, colours and shapes whizzing by. At the point where I begin to think that I am indeed capable of flight, I crash to the soft pink ground, with a dull, wet thud. Perhaps it's just the shock, or perhaps the actual pain, but I black out.

When the world comes back, the first thing I notice is the noise - industrial clanking whirring noise - beating to a steady rhythm; one, two, one, two.... Everything's out of focus. Nothing looks real. Hm. Concussion. Well, at least I tried. I stand up, and the various unidentifiable shapes begin to make sense. Or at least, as much as they can, under the circumstances.

A man stares down at me. The majority of his skull frames one huge globe of an eye - an eye concentrated on my body – which sits above a little button nose and reddish-purple lips (full, fleshy ones). He has no hair, facial or otherwise, and seems unnaturally skinny -

a childlike waif if it wasn't for his commanding stature. He just seems to be staring; I'm not sure if he's going to say anything. The background materialises behind him, and I remember where I am. Below me is a smallish pile of toys - a tiny robotic velociraptor is digging into my shoulder. It hurts, but I make no attempt to move, mainly due to the feeling I'm currently experiencing – sort of like my skin has thickened by about an inch and callused over. My whole body is swollen - or at least, it feels that way.

I worry that I won't to be able to understand the Cyclops-like man, but this fear is quelled when he speaks with a neutral, New England-style American accent. "You realise you came in the wrong way?" It's hard to tell, given his eyebrows blends into his scalp (it's a sort-of brownish-pinkish tone), but he sounds disapproving - clearly I've flouted some sort of rule. "You can talk, right? You're not, like, some fucked-up toy for some weirdo sadmasochist?"

I shake my head. No, I'm not a toy. He shakes his head back at me. "Wrong way, then. And you're late." At this point I remember what I'm here for - some sort of story. I sit up, my skin throbbing, and see a round table over away from the hustle and bustle of the factory floor, with a load of freaks sitting around it. I get up, and walk over. The man says "Don't thank me, then," and I don't.

I feel his sullen glare bore into me as I walk away. Or stumble, at least. I feel drunk. My arms flail, out of control. Nothing wild; just a general lack of control. The important details shrink, and the minute becomes magnificent. That said, it's hard not to notice the assorted slaves collecting presents, wrapping them, discarding the ones with manufacturing issues into piles like the one I ended up in. They all seem to have some genetic defect or other. A girl, smoking a cigarette, has nostrils stretching around her head, forming a parting around the back like little bullet holes, or the dashes on a cut line, like those cardboard toys you used to get on the back of cereal boxes. Another man's head is fused between his thighs, forcing his legs apart, while a bulge at the top of his jumper (sewn together at the neck) suggests genitalia.

There's a huge man, more stomach than body, blocking the way to the table. His eyes are currants - no metaphor, here, his eyes are actually dried up little husks of raisins. The rest of his features are virtually nonexistent, just slightly face-shaped smears of icing sugar. I'm not sure what to say to him; he definitely isn't letting me past unless I do something. But what do I do? I'm not sure whether or not to speak.

An interminable silence follows, only to be broken when I try and step around him. "Password," he says.

I'm perplexed, so I say the first word that pops into my head: "paedophile?" To my utter amazement, he steps aside. What am I getting myself into? And why was the first word that came to mind "paedophile"? Did I accidentally reveal some disturbing element of my subconscious?

I walk past, with a muttered 'thanks', and fill the only empty seat on the table. Here, I really do begin to reassess my definition of 'freak', for the various men and women I passed earlier look normal by comparison. On one seat appears to be a floating headless foetus with no skin, filling in a su doku puzzle with remarkable speed, surrounded by a long glass tank filled with some green fluid. If it wasn't alive and clearly sentient, I'd expect it to be found in a science museum. Sadly, this is one of the most ordinary-looking creatures on the table.

A great, hulking, fire-breathing spider with the head of Robert Downey Jr.; A paper aeroplane dragging its limp, lifeless tendrils along the table behind it, secreting something that burns through wood, reciting the latest stock market figures. And sat at the head of the table is a large, rotund-bellied red suit, trimmed with jagged razor-blades, all painted white. Below the table are a pair of black boots, with squares of frozen urine functioning as buckles. Streaming down the front of the suit, like some opaque waterfall, is milk - sour milk, giving off a pungent smell that makes me gag. The milk comes to a point somewhere around the suit's midriff, where it vanishes. From the top of the suit, the milk never seems to stop, spurting forth from the weirdest feature of all. Although there is no man inside this suit, there is definitely a man-shaped *something* - a furious cloud of static, never ceasing. Although it has no features, it appears to glare out at everyone seated - an empty, mechanical, ominous stare that makes me shiver.

In this reverie of confusion, I neglect to notice that all the background factory noises have stopped, and that the various workers have come and sat down around the table. I whirl around. They all look up to the table. For one horrifying moment, I think they might be looking at *me*, and I nearly lose control of my bowels. But then, I turn around again to face the others, and I see that the static has disappeared, to be replaced with the pixelated-looking face of a man gazing out. Or rather, what remains of one after serious poverty, drug abuse and sleep deprivation. Bloodshot eyes stare out, framed by eyebags so pendulous and black that they could be filled with tar. Dark, matted facial hair hangs off his sallow pinched cheeks; the cheekbones jut out of his face, providing ledges that his eyes seem to sit on. His hair, just visible below the conical paper hat of the suit, is sparse and limp, and he keeps having to wave away the odd stray lock out of his eyes. I know that he can't be physically here - partially due to the juddering in his movements and the fact that he appears as a high-tech version of a low-bandwidth internet video, but also because there is no way a man with such a haunted, empty face could fill the giant suit that sits beneath him. This must be a transmission from somewhere. This suspicion is only confirmed when the lights fade out to reveal his backlit form.

He clears his throat, hacks up some phlegm (which he spits off camera) and begins.

"Is this thing on?" he starts, tapping against a lens of some sort. People here and there murmur "yes." There is a muffled squawk in some far-off corner. He goes on. "Good, 'cause I haven't got long.

Uh, right, hang on." He disappears off-camera, treating us to the peculiar sight of a messy single man's bedroom - metal posters on the wall, used condoms lying around. In some drugged frenzy the word "FUCK" has been scrawled on the wall in what I hope is red pen, but looks more like blood. We hear the tinny rustling of paper, and his face fills the space again. "All still there?" His eyes dart back and forth. "Right. Here we go, then. Uh, I've called it 'A Christmas Tale Of Mystery And Joy', because I couldn't think of a decent title. Look, here it is...." He holds the piece of paper, showing the typewritten header "A CHRISTMAS TALE OF MYSTERY AND JOY, by Satan Klaus". He sounds drunk. He puts the sheet down again. "OK. Right. Any kids in the room?" The eyes dart around again. "Good. Here we go, then.

Once upon a time, it was Christmas. Christmas was mysterious as to why the *fuck* it was important, not to mention relevant to anything in modern-day society, but at the same time brought limitless joy to the millions of consumerist fucking morons who celebrated it. The End." And the face cuts out again, to white noise and rapturous applause. I blink. Is *that* what I came down here for? The cynical ramblings of a junkie? The applause doesn't stop - some are even whooping and cheering - and I begin to feel claustrophobic. I begin to budge through the standing ovation, but it proves difficult. Eventually, I resort to climbing over the factory workers' shoulders. They don't seem to notice, too fixed on their own delirious adulation. I finally reach the outside limit, and am about to climb into one of the moving carts pointing back the way I came in, when the applause suddenly stops. I turn slowly, and look at the crowd before me. They are all still looking towards the table, but now the suit is standing up. I notice that the legs have extended somewhat, making it about ten, maybe twenty feet tall. The face flickers back on, and it searches around. This time, he's slow, meaningful, looking for something. He says, slowly, but dripping with venom...

"Someone... has been... a NAUGHTY BOY."

The last time I heard those words, it was during a particularly violent lovemaking session, but there is no sexual overtone to this man's statement. The words are spoken with hatred, and by the way everyone breathes in sharply it's clear he means business. He keeps looking, until his eyes rest on one man. Me. "You," he says, and everyone turns to face me, shocked. "GET HIM!" he screeches, his face turning red. Instantly, the crowd burst into action. I do the only thing I can, under the circumstances.

I run.

The first place I look is the entrance to the glass tunnel leading back up to the oesophagus, but I nearly snap my fingers off when two thick steel shutters slam shut, blocking my escape. I look around frantically. The swarm gains on me, teeth bared, eyes aflame (where appropriate). My eyes scan the perimeter, and screech to a stop above some double doors with the header "EMERGENCY EXIT". It seems my best option. I run, as fast as my under-exercised legs will carry me. The crowd senses my change of direction and follows.

As I get closer, I see that the doors are made of some pulsating orange substance. I can't see a handle, or any sort of opening mechanism. A surge of confused panic serves as last minute energy, and I spurt forward. A bunch of childlike creatures, eyes gazing up at me dolefully, block my path. I smash through them, paying them no heed, sending them flying. I need to get out.

I finally reach the doors and claw around for some way to open them. The crowds close in. Panic rises in me again, engulfing me. In an animalistic frenzy, I run back a few steps, in the direction of the mob, then with all my might I run forward and barge into the door, and I dissolve through...

I crash to a bed of snow, and black out from the exhaustion.

I reawaken, to the sound of a horse whinnying and the clatter of footsteps. I blink the snow from my eyes, and I realise that I'm back. Back, in London, on the very street this all started, but in my own timeline. The man in the orange robes has gone.

Shakily, I get to my feet, and dust myself down. My entire right side has been soaked where the snow melted. I look behind me, expecting to see the double doors I smashed through, but instead I just see a shop selling toys and gifts, with the inscription "KLAUS & SONS: AT YOUR SERVICE" adorning the entrance.

I back away, slowly, and go home. I'm unsure of what I've learnt, but satisfied in the knowledge that the lesson itself was memorable enough to last me a lifetime.

Fired

Fuschia/725/Gamma-N - Frank to his friends – was walking – rolling, rather – across the busy street to the high rise. He was segregated, as were they. Humans on the right, arachnids on the left. It was preferable for everyone. No-one wants to make the morning commute surrounded by flesh-eating spiders. And the spiders had launched a national program to combat obesity. If they distanced themselves from food... well, everyone ended up happy.

Frank's legs had been missing for a long while. He missed them. One morning, he had woken up, and they had left, leaving a heartfelt letter of farewell at the foot of the bed. They hadn't said if (or when) they were coming back, which led to Frank buying his wheels. It had been difficult controlling them at first, but now that he was getting used to it he felt rather comfortable with his new status. Seeing people go past on their Segway scooters, he felt one step ahead of them.

Frank was going to a meeting at his place of work. This would be the first time he would see the CEO's office. He had become a deputy manager in the last couple of months, and this might be a promotion.

He glided into the lift, by now ignoring the stares from the various other businesspersons, and pressed the button for the 4035th floor. He garnered looks of surprise. No-one went to the top. No-one but him. He felt privileged.

The elevator flew up to the top floor in a jiffy, only pausing to let the commuters – more and more in awe of his status the higher the lift went – exit to their respective floors. It slowed to a halt, like an enthusiastic jelly bean reaching the airbag of a vacuum cleaner, let out an ambient fanfare to announce the arrival at his destination, and the doors opened.

There, in all his glory, was the CEO of the corporation. Old, but full of vitality. A strange quality to him - it appeared almost as if his skin was a separate entity to his body, taking on different expressions and qualities all the time. A quirk, maybe. He was known to have quirks. Frank rolled over, and leant against one of the beanbags which adorned the place. He would have sat, but to sit would have required a limb of which Frank was strangely deficient.

The CEO coughed, sniffed, and raised his eyebrows. He muttered under his breath an old nursery rhyme. Patta-cake patta-cake, baker's man, bake me ... he trailed off, looked up and feigned surprise at Frank's presence. This was followed by a stare that lasted a good minute, and then two words:

"You're fired."

Frank gaped. This he was not expecting. Not in the slightest. "Fired, your fatcatness?" *Your fatcatness* was the correct address for a man of such high position, and Frank *always* put propriety first.

"Yes, that's right. You've been compromising the productivity of our other workers by refusing to oil your wheels and squeaking all over the place. As a result, you're fired. Collect your things, and -"

The spider crawled over the CEO's back, now reaching round to pierce the neck and knock him out. It was large in stature, and of a deep brilliant, blue, byzantine texture, which shone a reflection onto the floor. Frank knew it was about to kill the CEO. He didn't know what to do. It was certainly a large spider - about two feet in diameter. He could try and kill the spider, but he would probably still be fired if the CEO survived. Or he could allow the spider to kill the CEO, in which case he would have the problem of a dead CEO and the liability of such a situation.

Eventually, after much literal tearing-out of hair and stress, Frank shouted "STOP!" and the spider did, just before its fatal stab.

Time passed.

A man who looked a lot like the CEO of the corporation sat in the chair. From a store cupboard in the office came a suspicious, munching, flesh-tearing noise, but the door was locked. If anything was indoors, be it files, folders, a corpse or a flesh-eating spider, it was not coming out soon. The CEO sat, smiling, rippling and swaying, a prisoner just getting used to his own skin, and he pressed the button for the switchboard.

"Send up Orange/929/Delta-B. I think I'm going to fire him."

He smiled.

Forgiveness

At the centre of the black spiralling cliffs, standing at the topmost point, arms spread as if on the cross, stood my mother, ready to jump.

I had been following her silently for months now, always keeping just out of sight. The path had been long and arduous. Underfoot was the sticky black tar that composed the whole cliff, sloping around and around, onward and upward, winding up to the endpoint - the point at which my mother now stood.

In addition to the terrible wind, a wind which threatened to throw me over either side, there was the roar of the surging plasma below, gaseous, fluorescent orange, boiling gloop that consumed anyone as soon as they stepped near.

And there, a hundred yards or so, off into the distance, perched my mother, about to relinquish her worldly body to the depths below. It was now or never. My clothes ragged and torn, billowing behind me, I made those final few steps and grabbed one of her outstretched arms. She didn't turn around, still facing the wind, tears of despair (or perhaps just a reaction to the extreme weather) running down her cheeks.

"Let go, Timothy," she said. I shook my head and tried to pull her away, but still she resisted.

"Why are you doing this?" I cried. "You have everything a human could want - a house, a family, a normal income, why has it come to this?"

"You know why," she whispered, her voice shaking. "This is your fault."

I sighed, dejected. "You know I didn't mean for any of this to happen." I tried once more to pull her away, but the exertion, coupled with the difficulty of lifting my feet up from the sticky floor proved too much to bear.

"You removed his head with a pair of garden shears, then painted a hundred smiley faces on his garden wall. With his blood. How can that not be deliberate?"

"I wasn't thinking straight, Mum! I was thinking immorally, but I've changed! I'm a new man! Look!" But she didn't look, and instead picked up her feet out of the quarter inch of tar encased around them, and jumped.

I was still holding on to her arm, and my grip tightened as she jumped, sending me down to the cliff face with a bone-cracking ferocity. My nose broke as my face hit the ground, and the tar branded my skin where it was uncovered, but I still held on, pulling as hard as I could.

I felt my muscles tearing. I looked down, over the side, and the sight of my mother against the burning bright plasma was such a contrast, her whole form was rendered a silhouette. I kept pulling, and realised that my efforts weren't wasted - I could feel movement, my sprawled body soon finding the capacity to shift backwards. I kept shifting, my arm on the verge of dislocation.

I nearly broke my grip when my skin began to tear, red muscle and blood showing beneath, accented by tendons straining with all their might, but I was nearly there and this sense of near-completion only drove me on, finally bringing her to the top once more.

I kneeled before her, mirroring her position, and bowed my head. And then, without warning, we began to cry, meeting each other's gaze with compassion, forgiveness, pity and desperation etched upon our faces. We leaned into each other, the cliffs stretching below us, a wild blur of orange against black, and held each other, the tears cascading down our faces in rivulets.

Before long, our eyes dissolved, replaced instead by gushing waterfalls of saltwater, neutralising the plasma below and filling the crevasses on either side. Our tears rose to the surface, pooling around our legs, then rising above our heads and we were drowning, fading from life together, locked in a final silent embrace, at peace.

Knives

I found myself in a rather distressing position. You can imagine how distressing walking along a busy high street, with fifty-three knives all jutting out of your midriff, whispering to you about how they've come to destroy the very fabric of time itself by slicing it up like a Sunday roast, while a crowd of onlookers stare at you, might be a little awkward. Possibly even embarrassing. Now imagine that this has just happened, giving you little - or, essentially, no - time to prepare for such an ordeal.

This is how I found myself. I wasn't sure what was more worrying - the police officers heading down the precinct, about to arrest me for obvious possession of multiple weapons, or the fact that these weapons could talk. The words that they were saying were "yeah, slice it up, all into nice little bite-sized pieces, ready to chomp like chicken nuggets." I hated chicken nuggets, and the idea of the fabric of time being reduced to this made me break out into a sweat. Now people were staring both at my armpits and my stomach. I felt naked. Naked, with knives sticking out of me.

At this most inopportune moment, the police officers decided to approach, tasers in hand, ready to shock me into submission. The first police officer shouted "SIR, DROP THE WEAPONS!" I couldn't exactly explain that they had fused to become part of my body, so I just stood there looking gormless while the other one shouted "YEAH!" I couldn't help but feel that this affirmation was a little unnecessary.

All the police had done was stir up anxiety. People were dropping to the floor like flies. Dead flies. Dead flies shot out of a cannon, straight into the ground. The knives were still talking, and getting more and more excited. "We's gunna BURN this world! Fiddle diddle with yer perceptions so you don't know who you are, where you are or when you are! You're gunna DIE, boys, screaming like liddle banshees! You scared?" I had to admit, I was more confused than scared. Or, if I was scared, it was that I was about to feel

10,000 volts surging through my body, and I'd have two identical electrical burns on my chest for the rest of my life.

"DROP THE WEAPONS, BITCH!" yelled the policeman. What the – had this turned into some gritty American crime show? Was I suddenly a gangster? Why the expletives? The second officer, who despite his larger stature seemed to be the other one's equivalent of tea boy, added to this glorious command by adding "YEAH, MOTHERFUCKER!" The sound of this coming from a twenty-year-old British mouth had the effect of me collapsing into girlish giggles.

Sadly, this sudden movement was mistaken for me reaching for a knife, but at that precise moment, the moment where I was to get toasted by the compact equivalent of a cattle prod, the knives decided to act and ripped the whole construct of the universe into a trillion tiny pieces, leaving nothing but renewed chaos for a whole new cycle of creation and destruction to form from.

And in that blink of a moment before they did, some scrap of sentient thought came to me from those destructive little objects, and that thought was that there is something very wrong about the concept of civilisation. But it didn't matter, because I was gone, torn into the fifty-three corners of the universe.

Mucus

The earth is warm. Long, dark grass leaps up before me, in this new great wilderness. I feel new. I *am* new – the entirety of me gets to know itself. Enzymes shake hands with other enzymes, the immunoglobulin huddles in a corner, not really trusting the rest of my composition but shyly wanting to help regardless. I am the mother of these creatures, and although my existence depends on theirs, I feel somewhat responsible for them in this new, mysterious world.

I try and move forward, but can't. So I wait, and in the meantime attempt to convert myself into a more fluid substance so I can move with more ease. This I do, and what was once a crusty old being that would move for no-one, now regresses back to some youthful state where I slide around my universe, gushing through the leaping brown roots, free. I feel like I could fly.

And then...

Blackout. What light was once here is gone, as the entrance to my cave is blocked. I panic, try to reform, but can't. Helpless, I flail around for something to hold onto, but every single blade of what was once a mysterious solace is slippery and useless. I feel something rumble from behind me, something that doesn't bode well. Then, without warning, a gale with the force of a thousand stampeding elephants smashes into me, sending my flying, splitting me off from the rest of my body, and I have to fight to stay conscious. Just when the terror begins to subside, I slam into the obstruction that blocks out the light, and the last thing I feel as I fade away into unconsciousness is that I'm being transported on some giant cushion of air.

A *thunk* awakens me, as I am dropped into a completely new surround. For a second, I'm blinded – the light here is so strong it takes a while to adjust. I see my new home – a series of white hills and contours, ending a few miles off with what just appears to be an abrupt stop. For a moment, I feel massively inferior, as if I've just been shown some universal truth.

And then I take in the whole scale of this world.

These hills, rather than being limited by an outer ring of nothingness, are merely the beginning. Beyond me, bright red tin glints temptingly, orange, bumpy pathways wind around and around, their tangy smell enticing me. Below me are light years of a new world, waiting to be explored. And above....

Above is a dazzling blue, too far off to touch, yet I feel at one with it without contemplation. White bubbles of candy floss drift across it, not in any rush, just waiting for the end of the world. A breeze tickles me, pushing me along my miniature landscape, as I slowly begin to lose my mind....

Peak

At the top of a hill, I pondered the meaning of the word 'peace', what it meant to me, and what it had meant to us.

The dystopian nightmare I had had since birth was being enacted before me. Skyscrapers crumbled to the ground. From all directions came the sound of screams. Even from my isolated standpoint, I could smell burning wood and flesh. Smoked meat. Even from my position, high above all this chaos, I could hear the individual screams of women and children – wails of anguish against the fiery night. I blotted out the sounds of the men. It's the sign of the world ending when men begin to cry.

I was alone, save for my pet meerkat (Ralf). As people had distanced themselves from me, I had grown more attached to Ralf. At least, I assumed it was that way round. I had begun talking to him. Ralf wasn't a deserter. Ralf couldn't comprehend the end of the world. I envied Ralf. Although, with my gift of foresight, I could see that the future wouldn't be so bad after all, despite this scene of utter destruction before me. Just – I'd rather have not had to think about it at all. The human characteristic of curiosity, if brought about by some omnipotent being, was a flawed one. Thinking took up too much time.

I closed my eyes, and returned myself to the vision of years to come. One by one, the screams would stop. The buildings would stop smoking, and the red fiery clouds would dull once more, then dissipate to reveal the azure of yesteryear. People would stare up at the sky, maybe for the first time in their lives, and stop panicking. There would be a global epiphany – not a religious kind, just a common realization of a better way to live one's life. One by one, the pieces would be picked up and thrown on the fire. People would finally live as one communal being. Knowing this, and hearing the sounds of death outside, I was reminded of a phoenix. This sound that so many mistook to be the end – crunching metal, the splash of running feet against rivers of blood – was merely the overture. The symphony was due to begin, but people hadn't yet taken their seats. I had, and so had Ralf. We knew what we were doing.

Peace, then – could peace really be seen as an ideal? I thought, staring out at the smoke, is it worth striving towards peace? After all, it's only ever come about by accident... Ralf had never striven towards absolute ideals, and he was by far the most peaceful creature I knew. My parents, friends, neighbours – they all had a *concept* of tranquillity, and wanted it more than anything, but their lives were wracked with turmoil and stress.

The city was a phoenix, burning up in a glorious cacophony of fire and rage. I reasoned that maybe all that the phoenix was, was the anthropomorphised equivalent of history: beautiful while it lasts, but a hair's breadth away from its own destruction. And out of those ashes, something more beautiful would be reborn, time and time again.

I lay back, and slept, whiling away the hours, days, months until this beautiful – but temporary – utopia would emerge. I could wait.

Peanut Cream

The new drug was called Peanut Cream, and it had taken London by storm. Everyone was addicted. Charlie, junk, weed, these were all bygone archaisms of yesteryear. Peanut cream was the hippest thing to be on, and the best thing about it was that there was no downer, no flooring, crushing depression once you came off it.

Sonny Boy George Vauxhall Unitarian Carmichael Smith was lying in a pile of binbags down an alleyway somewhere around Edgware Road, strapping up with a belt and a syringe he had found in a drinks fountain in Hyde Park. He had eight mils of *larasheed*, the latest mix, ready to push into his veins. Rats sniffed around his feet, which were clad in a pair of rundown old brown boots, worn from years of ambling around the festering city of bureaucrats and Satan-worshipping merchant bankers, trying to find meaning. He hoped that this groovy new drug would be the answer. He had tried every drug under the sun, was a raving alcoholic for a decade or so but had just found it a waste of time. Everything grew boring sooner or later, and this was his problem - an interminable *ennui* with everything he went anywhere near. He was beginning to think that it was his fault - that he *made* things boring - and such a thought was incredibly depressing. He had contemplated suicide, but had grown bored of thinking about it.

Peanut cream looked exciting - it radiated a warmth uncommon to most drugs, and despite its creamy-beige colour seemed to dazzle when one looked at it. He lowered the filthy syringe into the bag and drew a few droplets out. It hung there, suspended, begging to be crammed into his veins. He obliged, lifting his leg and jabbing the needle into the soft bit behind his knee (the standard form of intake).

He waited. The effects were supposed to include a huge rush of euphoria, followed by a feeling of being completely at peace with the universe. These feelings didn't surface. Instead, he felt nothing. But then -

As he went to get up, his entire body spasmed, sending him back down into the garbage below. He tried getting up again; the same happened. This couldn't be normal - a ceaseless attraction to refuse couldn't possibly be the reason why everyone was on it. Then, he heard - and felt - a large cracking noise down his spine. No - wait - not *down* his spine, but *around* it. Something was forming....

Before he had a chance to cry out, his veins suddenly ripped out of his face and body, propelled outward by some magnetic force, tearing his skin into a million tiny pieces as each individual capillary hardened in contact with the air. His entire mass was multiplied by ten, each blood vessel - in his feet, his eyes, everywhere jutted out at a ninety-degree angle to its previous position. Now rock solid, the ends of each capillary, already splurting blood, congealed to produce a massive clot around him, blacking out his already failing vision. The last thing he saw was each vein, each artery turning the colour of light brown....

Four years later. Vagrants walk the city of London, perplexed, wondering what they missed. Everywhere they look, giant human-sized peanuts leer out from every office, every alleyway. Times Square is the worst, littered with kernels piling sky-high. A ghost town of nuts. They wonder: *what happened? How? Who will serve me at McDonald's? Who will I go to when I want my footlong Italian BMT from Subway? Who will serve me my caramel cream frappuccino in Starbucks? Who will show me to my seat when I see Fame - incidentally, a musical acted entirely by completely static man-sized nuts?* These previous convenience consumers, desperate for a commercial fix, have no idea what to do. No-one is coming to rescue them; London has become a secluded, ignored city, as everyone is too confused by the situation to act. So, starving, desperate and baffled by this new microcosm of existence, the miniscule population wander around, occasionally taking a bite out of the peanuts that aren't too dirty, aren't too... *person*-like.

Down an alleyway, somewhere around Edgware Road, beneath a heap of untouched binbags, something rustles.

Room Ninety-Three

Raphael opens the door.

His hand rests briefly on the doorknob, feeling its solid oak contours, a rounded ball of fury, accented with six lines, forming a smooth hexagonal prism. He breathes in. The room behind him has gone - if he looked back, which he knows never to do, then he would see nothingness. Not darkness, but nothing. And Raphael knows better than to stare into nothing. He's seen men do it before, and go insane just from the act itself.

As usual, Raphael doesn't know what is beyond the door, hence his hesitancy. He is allowed to proceed at whatever speed he feels necessary, but he is never allowed to look at his past. Live in the moment, they said. Everything in your past is dust, they said. There is no such thing as achievement. There is no such thing as personal development. There is only the now, they said. They are always saying this. They need to, if Raphael is going to follow them. He is all too aware of the paradox of living in the present based on the advice of someone from the past.

He hears the latchbolt click as it slides away from the jamb. There is the sound of wood against steel, dull, solid, marked with a full stop. He pushes, lightly, and the whole panel scrapes as it struggles to break free of its binds. And then...

An Indian man playing a sitar, his knuckles decorated with parrot skulls, heavily made-up with darkened eye-makeup, but stylishly, beckons Raphael in, the caramel walls offering false warmth to him. The man doesn't take his eyes off him, but carries on playing the sitar as an array of instruments join him, blaring out from a series of megaphones, each one balancing on a purple cushion.

Raphael crosses the room, and sees an empty cushion. He looks at the sitar player. He nods, apprehensive.

The sound of crushed parrot skulls on a bed of silk distracts him for a moment, and he looks down to his bandage-swaddled feet to see that this is what he is stepping on. A thousand bird skulls, each one condemned never to feel the rush of air ever again.

Raphael tiptoes across the room, hoping not to crush any of the tiny avian crania, but failing due to the bulky footwear forced upon him a hundred years ago.

He sits down.

And he begins to sing.

Skydiver

You jump.

And you begin to fall. The wind rushing past you. You're already picking up speed, and you've only just left the plane. You remember what the instructor told you. Don't look up. Look up, and you'll break your neck. Eyes on the ground. You want to look up. You want to see the aeroplane disappearing above you. But you don't.

Around this point, you wish you'd got a haircut. Your hair covers your face. Shouldn't you be wearing a cap, or something? You got the goggles, but they don't exactly make you feel safe. Or comfortable. You gnash your teeth, and accidentally tear out a few follicles with the sheer power of your jaw. You're feeling strong. Liberated. The sky is your only companion.

The air resistance begins to pick up. The wind nips against your face. It begins to sting. Smart, even. It feels like your face is soaked in some gaseous blood - your face is boiling up, you can feel each vein adjusting. There's a moment of panic - you don't want to have your face covered in some veined mass when you get back to earth. Vain? Probably.

Your instructor nods to you, and you pull the cord. The parachute billows out behind you. You wonder when it's supposed to slow you down. Your instructor looks at you, yelling something, but you can't hear him. The wind's too loud. You smile. This is beginning to feel good, like you're on some caffeine buzz.

Then you look up, and you see why you haven't felt any sort of yank from the parachute. Someone's cut the cords. At this point, you look round, and your neck snaps round with excruciating pain. You can't move your neck back, so your head's concentrated on your back. Eight protruding cords, flapping aimlessly. The parachute drifting lazily above, where you should be. Your instructor waving his arms. He's having a panic attack. Why? He's safe.

With a gross amount of effort, you force your head back round to the earth below. Your heart's thumping. You begin to count in time: one, two, one, two... it's probably at this point that the full mental force of your impending death hits you. You cry. You scream. You flail. The tears steam up the goggles. You can't see anymore.

And perhaps it's this that stops you. Just one of your senses has gone, but that feels safe to you. All that fear, that worry, it's gone, and you solemnly and expectantly await your death. You think: *there are worse ways to die*, whilst all the time knowing that what you're thinking is probably insane. But it doesn't matter.

You think of Charles Darwin on his deathbed.

The Pit of Technological Chaos

At the peak of the volcano, two men - strangers up until this point - were staring down, observing what lay within. The less intelligent of the two raised his gaze to meet the other's.

"What do you suppose it is?" he said, trying not to notice that the other man's entire body was melting due to the intense heat from the volcano. This was not an easy act to perform, as men in a liquefying state often cannot help but be noticeable. Neither, notably, can they speak, so the man who was melting communicated through telepathy: *this is the pit of technological chaos.* His suit caught fire.

The less intelligent man looked down once more, and began to see shapes emerging. Large, robotic figures, propelled by what appeared to be the evaporated blood-steam of a mass of churning bodies within each one, were lolling about, occasionally striking one another but with no real malicious intent. A mass of machines, reduced to aimlessness, dwelling in a churning lava pit.

"When?" asked the less intelligent one, for even *he* knew that beyond the mouth of the volcano lay the representation of a different time. The melting man, whose eyes were now running down the sides of his face in two symmetrical lines, fired his thoughts over from his mind-cannon: *the twenty-ninth century.*

The less intelligent man said, "It's safe to go down there?" The last thought the other man had before collapsing into a puddle of blood and bones was *don't*, but by this point it was too late; the less intelligent man had begun to climb down.

It was a peculiar detail that the one remaining man was not boiling to death, but he had at least had the good sense to invest in a hand-woven costume containing lizard skin and solid nitrogen before climbing the volcano, and as such was currently descending at what he felt was a reasonable, if a little stuffy, room temperature.

Like the other man (who was picking up pace as he slid down the sides, mixing with the lava to create a sort of symbiosis, the effect of which would eventually scare a passing tourist to death) the descending man was wearing a business suit on top of his frozen-lizard protective layer. It was tailored, and a vivid blue, with a red tie. He had been told the two colours went together, and for this reason he had worn it today.

He crossed through the time field, making a loud 'thwock' noise as the last part of his head went through, and hopped onto a curiously sturdy platform along the side of the volcano. Straight ahead of the man, embedded into the volcanic wall, was a glass front panel, adorned at the centre by a double door proclaiming it as the residence of a Mikael K. Pietersen. The less intelligent man pressed the buzzer to get in. The buzzer screamed back at him. To spite it, he pressed it again, and this time the buzzer let out a confused, tiny whimper, and the man heard a 'click' which meant he was invited inside. For a moment, when the door was closed, he turned back to see the robots. One had turned to face the glass fronting, and the man could see inside the robot's translucent shell a churning mass of people, like disjointed veins. Occasionally, one would explode into a million bloody crystals, and each one would fire out of the robot's pores, propelling it in yet another direction. The man became transfixed by this, not noticing that his benefactor, the aforementioned Mikael K. Pietersen, had come down to greet him.

He turned around, and Mr. Pietersen was standing directly in front of him, having just descended a marble staircase that could not have feasibly been built within the volcano's walls. He was extending his hand in welcome, and the man shook it, falling to his knees. He had waited a long time for this, and his moment had finally come.

The Plum'b

The great bodiless plum'b hung there before me, the mental projection of itself pendulous, like so many collected raindrops. I quivered. Neither of us had spoken yet. The plum'b had called me here, to this dank little cave, late last night. After all it had done for me, I could hardly refuse. But as to why it had called me down here, I was as clueless as the next man.

It began to produce a sound I had not before heard - the sound of a million perishing dolphins, wrapped in a breathless paper film of ice, repeatedly thrumming out a slow, barely discernible beat. The sound was simultaneously calming and headache-inducing. Then, as this effect took place, I remembered - I had heard this before, when I had first been rescued by the plum'b. What's more, I knew what was coming next, and covered myself just in time.

As if vomited from the mouth of a giant, a waterfall of blue, glittering bile cascaded from above, flecked with milky-white moments that made me think of fluoride, gushing over and around my head as I lay in the foetal position, my arms wrapped around my skull. Fear throbbed through me, in part because I knew what was about to happen. I was going to start breathing again, sooner or later, and the bile would inevitably catch in my throat. I would flail, and panic. And I would drown. And then... it had only happened once before, and even now I couldn't remember.

This all began to occur. On the cusp of asphyxiation, I gasped for breath, as a huge glob of the plum'b's bile leapt down my throat and stuck in the middle of my oesophagus, some sticky little membrane lying in wait for a challenge. And along they came - drops here and there, but soon a steady trickle of bile meandered down my throat, as I faded away from life...

The plum'b stood before me. Its million shapes simultaneously became known to me. I swooned, but stayed conscious. The plum'b smiled, with a billion years behind the expression.

"Thank you," I whispered.

Wakey Wakey

Michael awoke to discover that his skull was being eaten by his alarm clock. This was not the first time it had happened this month. Rather, it was becoming rather predictable. Somewhere over the previous Christmas, his alarm clock had acquired the ability to mould itself around his cranium, and had grown teeth to boot.

The only consolation that Michael had was that the bite of his alarm clock was not particularly strong, so he was able to remove it from his brain with only a few mild indentations in his skin.

Or rather, this had been the norm up until recently.

This very dawn, Michael only delighted in the morning sun for a few seconds, before the alarm clock, infused with energy from a combination of solar rays and a leftover Toffee Crisp, bit clean through Michael's skull and feasted on his brains.

This isn't as gruesome as it sounds. So quick was the incision, and so deep was the alarm clock's suction of his various fluids into its innards, that there was barely a drop of blood spilt. In addition, the first bite of the alarm clock severed the pain receptors in Michael's head, so he didn't suffer.

What now remained was an alarm clock, suspended on half of Michael's head. The eyes, ears, and his beautiful head of hair had been consumed. Most of his nose had gone, but his nostrils - squashed underneath the clock's base - remained, as did his mouth and the normal morning stubble.

Michael, or the clock possessing Michael, got up and went downstairs to get some breakfast. His new clock mind settled on Crunchy Nut Cornflakes. It was clear from this that the clock had different priorities to Michael - he had always preferred Coco Pops. Such disturbing changes.... His new mind felt it apt to wolf down the cereal, and this he did.

There was the remembrance of something - perhaps Michael's brains were diffusing through time - and Miclock, Clochael, this new creature did for a moment glance wistfully over at the cupboard to where the Coco Pops lay untouched. He considered a second course, but felt this too extravagant.

Michael burped, with a barely-audible beep, and left the house.

The Life and Times of Paul Lincoln

Prologue

We live in an abandoned old house on a street of abandoned old houses. There's me, and there's Bradley, my grandson. Beautiful boy. All the more so when you think about the world out there. I cry sometimes at night when I think about what he must make of it all.

An entire nation, reduced to rubble in the space of a year. Of course, I was a kid at the time. I saw the worst of it. The feral screeching at all hours of the night, the martial rule, the mass indiscriminate exterminations... I saw it all, and thankfully only understood half of it. I say thankfully – I took images with me that I didn't understand at the time, but years later wake me up in a cold sweat.

No-one really knows how it happened. One day, Working London's one of those places you don't think twice about, an ignored country below your feet, then the next... chaos.

It started in London. I know. Typical. Overnight, there was a mass breakout from one of the slums – and when I say mass breakout, I mean hundreds of thousands. God knows how. Some people say that they had help from outside – communist sympathisers, that sort of thing. Some say that they just went from docile to possessed in a night – that the fortifications in place to hold them suddenly weren't enough. But either way, they broke out, and they realised the lie we'd built for them, and this just tripled their anger.

Imagine a hundred thousand people suddenly driven mad, let loose on a major city. In the first week, hundreds died. There was no method, and no discrimination. On the news, we saw images of kids torn to pieces. That was the turning point for me. That was the week I realised I was glad that my wife had died of cancer. It sounds awful saying that, even ten years on, but I am – because they would have got her, and that would have ruined me. I'd be reduced to the level of a jabbering crazy person, just like the others.

Of course, some of the escapees had a method to their madness. Like some collective intuition, they found all the entrances, and dispersed over the country to let them out. It took them a while, but with an immobilised police force, they could do whatever they wanted. The only people left were vigilantes, and... well. I'm not sure what it is about the British, but we just don't do vigilante justice.

Imagine a tidal wave crashing into your house. Awful, isn't it? Now, imagine that same tidal wave, but instead of water, it's made of people. And when it rolls back, some of the same people are there, but there's also people from your house, your street. And they're all dead.

Extending the metaphor: me and Bradley, we clung onto the driftwood. His parents and sister died, bless them. Besides that, we've got no-one. Or we think we haven't – either way, since we moved to the capital we're in a community of about 3,000. The capital of the country, and three thousand is all we can muster up.

Don't get me wrong – it wasn't just a straightforward massacre, though the death toll when the entirety of Working London was let out was nightmarish, more than you could believe. No – everything went downhill when they left. The UN, already considering us to be suspect of mass criminal activity, effectively quarantined the country. Gunships were permanently placed at strategic points to stop people from leaving. We'd created an underground prison for our own people – now the rest of the world was giving us a taste of our own medicine. With no more imports and exports, starvation was an issue, and of course suicide rates went through the roof.

Eventually, the dust settled, and we tried to struggle on. Of course, with no-one working underground, we had to start from scratch – London's closer to a city-state now than it used to be, with different people allotted to farming, or power generation, or construction.

The last one's laughable – people rooting through the debris, trying to find suitable building materials. The rest of the world just looked on and laughed.

This was our punishment for two hundred years of unique but corrupt ideology, and they just looked on and laughed.

Chapter One

I swung out of Blackfriars-Mason Law Offices, my head bare to the light drizzle descending from above. I looked up. Beautiful, voluminous clouds, like hazy zeppelins, hung overhead, shifting inch by inch with every passing second. Below me, at the bottom of the fifteen steps to the door I had just exited through, was a flurry of movement; men and women rushed back and forth, umbrellas clattering into each other, getting tangled, becoming the subjects of tiny scuffles, disputes and chance encounters here and there. I looked up again, blinking back the rain from my already-drenched face. I let my hands run through my slick black hair, plastered to my skull, fingers shifting down past my cheekbones to the point of my chin. I breathed in, my lungs inflating to full capacity, the crisp autumn air refreshing my pores. Magnificent.

Today had been a good one. The Lündstrom case had been a success. The man who raped Ms. Lündstrom and killed her brother had, with my help, received two life sentences, with no time off for good behaviour. In my own way, I felt like a superhero. Here was a grossly ineffectual system, and I was tweaking it a little so that filth like her abuser would never see the light of day again. I had become, in my own quaint manner, a force for good. And I loved it.

Already soaked to the skin, I skipped down the steps and joined the hustle and bustle of the inner city. My suit clung to me, but I didn't care. Nothing could put me in a bad mood today.

As always, I savoured the walk home – two miles in total – while everyone else rushed off to the nearest tram to take them down the road half a mile. Beetles in matchboxes, they reminded me of. I, on the other hand, preferred to enjoy the fresh air.

My journey home took me through Hyde Park, down Oxford Street and then off to the right. Hyde Park was in a forgotten area of London – an immediate leap into the suburbs. I couldn't help but marvel at the rest of the world, and its gross, sprawling monsters of cities. I had seen videos of Manhattan, in particular, and couldn't help but marvel at how a city so concentrated could sprawl out so far. Of course, we had an entire underground equivalent of every city - technically, I lived in Upper London, as opposed to just straight 'London', but Working London was our dirty little secret that no-one liked to give too much of a voice to. But despite the grumbling underground world of vice, squalor and poverty, I wouldn't want to live anywhere else but here. Give me London – five square miles of the city, framed by another fifteen or so of suburbia, then the sweet English countryside, perfect in its simplicity.

To return to Hyde Park, I was trying to keep to the narrow grit path, but all to no avail – my boots were covered in mud. I sighed in satisfied resignation. It didn't matter. In this lush, green common, a mile and a half long but with only me gracing its carpet of grass, no-one was going to see the mess I was becoming. I picked at my shirt, prising it away from my skin. It smacked back again, sending a chill through my chiselled body. The rain was getting heavier. I quickened my pace and decided to remove my shades, given that the rain had created a film over them that made it impossible to see.

Scrunching up my eyes, as I did on every occasion the sunglasses came off, I pushed past the various brambles and entered into the trees. A crack and a flash filled the air. Storm. I moved on, despite the tempting shelter of the lichen-covered overhead canopy. Finally, I pushed through the gate and exited the park onto the empty street. The beginning of (Upper) Oxford One – a quarter of the Oxford Street neighbourhood. Usually, given the general absence of automobiles here, I would walk down the centre of the cobbled street. Pavements relegate the pedestrian to a substandard position. Walking along the middle of the road, one becomes king of it, to paraphrase some long-forgotten folk song. Today, however, with the rather impractical footwear adorning my feet (rule of the courtroom number twenty-three: dress to impress), I opted to stick to the pavement; the cobbles were each just a slippery hazard to my health. Best to be avoided in this weather.

Victorian gas lamps still lit the streets. Perhaps that's why I loved my area – it retained a level of old-world charm, a sense of non-motorised peace and quiet that was perfectly suited to me, given that I was a child of both worlds. That's right – I'd become snobbish about my roots over the years, but below me was Working London, my birthplace. Specifically, the term was Working Kensington Six, but as the network of streets and pathways was vastly different underground to up on the service, the name was to some extent irrelevant – it just served as a reference point for us in the 'real' London, Upper London. I could never remember much of my Working childhood, but what I did recall made me happy that my memory was so limited. Twelve years of my life, wilfully obliterated by my mind.

I know everyone around here. Mr. Rowbotham, the archaeologist at No. 5; Annabel Smythe, a girl I had been eyeing up for a couple of months now; the Cheung family, wealthy immigrants from China but seamlessly integrated into the neighbourhood; each had their own distinctive quality that helped me remember them. Don't get me wrong – Oxford Street was by no means a small road, hence the need to split the neighbourhood into four distinct parts – but I at least knew everyone in Oxford One, and certainly a few in Oxford Two.

My road – Warwick Road – was more of a dirt track, each house a couple of floors high with a picket fence running down the whole street, framing the front gardens. During the summer, Warwick Road became idyllic – kids playing in the streets, people enjoying a glass or two of wine (or a tumbler of Scotch for me) on the porch. I was the only inner-city professional on the road, but I preferred to keep it that way. Here was an ignored area where I could escape from the heavy, money-grabbing cynicism of my colleagues. A nice little contrast to be greeted with at the end of the day. My neighbours had initially regarded me with suspicion – I was a City boy, not to be trusted – but as they realised I had the same ultimate ideals as them (peaceful living, communion with nature, that hippie nonsense) they soon warmed to me.

The rain was stopping, and I began to feel the chill. It was getting dark, too, the clouds above acting as some strange filter to the light of the sun behind them, casting a dull yellow glow over everything. Autumn sunset, fleeting but breathtaking. I drew the air in through my teeth, expelling it through my nostrils. I blinked back the rain, just like before, casting away the stray droplets clinging to my eyelashes – little reminders of the journey home.

Nearing the gate to my driveway, I heard a familiar yell. "Afternoon, Paul!" rang the voice of Samuel, my neighbour from Alabama. It was simultaneously refreshing and cloying, having an American living next door to me: refreshing, as Sam's scruffy, laid-back, surprisingly liberal attitude made a change from the bourgeois semi-conservatism of the other residents, but cloying given that Sam was in every respect a stereotype, down to the cowboy hat and dungarees. You could have plucked out a farmhand from Texas and put them side by side, and the only thing distinguishing them would be that Sam advocated free love and cannabis use, while the Texan would probably be against all pleasures apart from sex with farm animals and his close family. Or so I was told. I'd never been to America. No need – I had everything I wanted right here.

I stopped short of opening the gate, and turned around. He was completely dry; he had obviously only just come out of his house, probably with the sole intention of saying hello. I turned, offered a subtle yet warm smile, and walked up the steps to my home.

I reached inside my briefcase for my keys. I never carried anything in my suit pockets; partially because it made them bulge unnaturally, thus ruining my otherwise clean-cut look; partially because the pockets were more for decoration than storage and hence were not particularly strong; but mainly because in the event of rain (or any inclement weather, for that matter), anything in those pockets would instantly be soaked. That said, my keys were never going to suffer any permanent damage... apart from maybe rusting... moving on. I reached around (in my briefcase, if you've forgotten), but neither heard nor felt the familiar metallic jangle of my keys. Worried, this casual exploration soon became a scrabble, but all to no avail: they had gone. Cursing, I remembered, with angry yet resolute defeat, that I had left them on my desk at work. Praying that they would still be there when I returned the next day, I descended the steps down from the porch and walked down to the alleyway at the back of the house. I was fairly sure I'd left the kitchen window open. True, I wouldn't look as dignified, but as I began to shiver I felt that such a trivial matter was less than important. All I wanted right now was a hot shower, a change of clothes and a steaming mug of tea.

I lived alone. I preferred it that way. Being single granted me more versatility. My nature as an immigrant (albeit a naturalised one with full citizenship) from Working London meant I was subject to rigorous monthly checks, ranging from the fiscal to the medical, and a permanent presence of a woman or man in my life would mean a lot of complications, beginning with a lot of unwelcome intrusions into their life as well as mine. I preferred to drift from partner to partner, having highly-charged emotional encounters. The lithe Miss Smythe was the latest object of my affections. She knew it, too, but was keeping me at a distance – to tease me, probably. Slowly, but surely, though, I was insinuating myself into her life – a chance meeting at a dinner party here, a drunken cab ride home there – and I guess it was all a little futile, when I considered that eventually I would be forced to leave her.

I turned the corner onto the narrow alleyway. People rarely came down here. It was only really wide enough for one and a half people, and so was only ever traversed by the odd tramp – and stupid buggers who had left their keys at work.

Doors were set in small alcoves every fifteen yards or so, each lit again by a singular hanging gaslight, casting strange shadows against me and the rapidly-darkening sky. I began to count down.

My house was right at the end of the road, and the alleyway was a dead-end; beyond the obvious back doors to each house's garden, there was only one entrance and exit. I lived at number twenty. Two, four, six... I smiled. I hadn't been down here in a while. Eight, ten, twelve... behind one of the doors – I couldn't tell which – I heard the croak of a crow, followed by hurried footsteps. Fourteen, sixteen, eighteen –

"Hold it."

A deep baritone voice came from behind me. I froze. Police? But I hadn't done anything wrong. As for muggers and robbers, crime was at an all-time low. I would have to be horribly unlucky to fall victim to any one of them. Frantic possibilities circled my brain, halting suddenly when I heard a gut-wrenching *click* and the cold, hard feeling of steel pressing against my skull.

"On your knees." I obeyed. There are a lot of things I'd do with a gun pressed to my head. Call me submissive, but you'd probably do the same. My legs, now all but dried out, were soaked again as they hit the freezing wet mud. I'd been shivering for a while, but this involuntary, continuous shudder was now intensified by the fear coursing through my mind.

The moment before he pulled the trigger, I'll be absolutely honest, even if it does satisfy the cliché – my life, in all its 27-and-a-half years, flashed before my eyes. Not a nicely planned narrative, though, but a jumbled, nonsensical mess – like I was experiencing every feeling I had every gone through, reliving every moment of my lifespan. Humiliation, pride, joy, despair, passion, apathy – they were all there.

At the same time that I remembered my fourth girlfriend stepping out of the shower, I was shaking hands with Michael Blackfriars, my employer. At the same time I was fighting past my closest childhood friends so I could grab a handful of swill, I was breaking up a fight between my work colleague, Peter, and a burly-looking man in a string vest in a local bar. For one beautiful moment, I felt omniscient in my own little universe, causing an inexplicable feeling of near-schizophrenia – anguish and elation poured out of me in equal torrents.

The slime of the mud below me, previously causing me huge discomfort, now refreshed me. The incessant thrumming in my temples become a strange form of therapy. As my killer squeezed the trigger, I could feel every millimetre that their finger shifted.

At the last second, I felt a sudden realistic surge of resolve. This was a cowardly way to die, murdered by someone I couldn't even see. I whirled around to face them, hoping I would reveal some huge mystery. And there, past the barrel of the gun, up the forearm, past the biceps clothed in leather, past a pair of symmetrical, perfect shoulders, was the face of a man. A chiselled, beautiful face. Dark eyes. Neutral expression. Cheekbones, powerful ones.

I had never seen this man before in my life.

The last thing I felt before I was killed was absolute bewilderment. I didn't protest. Didn't cry out, lose control of my bowels, nothing like that. All there was, were questions. *Why? What had I done? Who was this man?*

And before I could ask any, with the gentle hiss of a silencer, I died.

Chapter Two

As the sun rose on a hot August morning, the Prime Minister of the United Provinces of Britain and Ireland was rubbing the sleep out of his eyes, stretching his arms, glancing over to the bed where his wife was soundly sleeping, and getting up. He glanced at the clock on the wall, and cursed himself for getting up too early – again. The little hand clicking softly into place at the number six, he lazily pulled on a dressing gown and descended downstairs.

As he walked down, he wondered what had caused this latent insomnia. Perhaps it was his wife's snoring... but she had always snored, and it had never been a problem in all of their twenty-five years of marriage. Perhaps the weather – an all-time high temperature of 41°C that summer, and they were still getting away with saying that humanity's extinction wasn't inevitable. But there was air conditioning in every room of the house, thank God. No – more likely, it was the job. Pressure had been mounting on him for some time to do something about the increasing unrest, but from the least likely origin. This wasn't the latest batch of econuts complaining about the New British Summer, or one of the borderline cults preaching illegally (it was said that in isolated parts of the country, Christianity was once more gaining a foothold). No, this time the unrest came from Working London – indeed, Working Britain in general. It wasn't necessarily a case of people demanding equal rights – by now, Upper Britain was regarded one of those mythical places, passed on only by the elderly and the odd glimpse of government officials and the delivery trucks. Once, they were seen as positively messianic, but now people were getting curious. There wasn't exactly a struggle for equal rights, but they wanted to be able to have their curiosities satisfied.

Today was the day his decisions on how to combat the problem would be put into effect. Over the last few months, it had been distributed via word of mouth that people would be allowed into Upper Britain, and this was true – in a sense. One young person was to be selected and granted full citizenship of the world above ground, in a trial run, and after that an immigration lottery would be set up. Of course, they would radically overexaggerate the figures – the underground consisted of hundreds of isolated communities, separated by rock, so even one individual or family emigration would be seen as fortuitous. In fact, there would only be five or six a year, but they weren't to know that – they'd just think they were unlucky. And this was the best way. The government couldn't allow the country to be overrun with vermin – not in a state with a right-wing voter percentage of 89%, where people were happy to be equal as long as it didn't affect them.

The Prime Minister hoped it would work, and it had no reason not to – things were just fine now, and the difference would be negligible. That, of course, was the other reason – this was his third term in office, and despite the stress of the job he liked where he was. He didn't want to do anything that'd endanger his status.

With no-one around at such an early hour to cook him his full English, he poured a bowl of Frosties and began to distractedly munch on them. Today's agenda was to begin at eight. Beyond that, the details were left to his personal aide, Roberts, who would arrive at about 7:30 with the rest of his staff.

The house was silent, save for the low hum of the central heating coming to life. He pushed the empty bowl of cereal away and began to absent-mindedly drum his fingers on the table. What he did know about today was that he was scheduled for an official visit to Working London. He was one of the few recognisable authority figures in Working Britain – while it was officially run in exactly the same way, the underground civilians each deferred to a state-appointed representative – 140 communities across the Provinces, all with their own Supreme Leader. Above ground, these representatives were simply MPs, but the underground wasn't to know that – they needed a proper authority figure, someone to keep them in check.

As he lived there, the Prime Minister was appointed Supreme Leader of Working London, and today he was due the full tour – the slums, one of the mess halls and the amphitheatre was planned. He had no real wish to see any of them, of course – but the people of Working London saw this as a momentous occasion, and he was there to add a bit of grandeur. Working England, Scotland and Wales (Ireland had its own governing body more bent on mutual cooperation than subjection to British rule) were all officially considered separate countries from their Upper Counterparts, with different laws and – in respect of their titles and powers – different leaders, so any state visit was regarded as a big diplomatic event. Of course, despite this distinction the underground was far from autonomous; Upper Britain still effectively owned the towns and cities below them, but recognising Working Britain as a separate state gave the government of those above a few useful advantages – such as immediate deportation and "medical treatment" of the odd escapee who crossed "state borders", and the removal of certain UN sanctions, who had previously condemned the Prime Minister for depriving human rights to his own citizens. Now, Working Britain was just like any third-world country – only the people below were controlled by the independent country above them.

He flicked the TV on from where he was sat and it flickered to life with The News Channel. Presenters always looked a little more haggard at this time of the morning, given that they had usually been reporting the same stories on repeat for the last six hours or so, full in the knowledge that hardly anyone was watching. They were still covering an underground rally in Working Manchester from yesterday. A man named Stephen Dobbs, who had escaped ten years ago, had suddenly and unexpectedly regained his memory and was ranting at anyone who would listen about everything Upper Britain was keeping from them. SWAT teams had already been sent to execute him in his sleep, but it had been an unsettling couple of weeks as the news emerged. The presenters, on the other hand, seemed apathetic more than anything about the story.

Now thoroughly depressed, he flicked the TV off, only to be confronted once again by the numbing silence. The PM was at a loss of what to do, and eventually resolved to freshen up for the day ahead. His outfit had been prepared the night before, and would take a little longer to put on – given that the mentality of Working London, despite men like Stephen Dobbs, was fixed fairly firmly in the 19th century, his suit was all-out pomp, bordering on ridiculous. It was still considered fitting down below that a leader should wear a top hat, and this was propped up on a stand next to his walk-in wardrobe. There had been occasions where previous government officials had gone below in their normal attire, and on every single event the level of mistrust had been terrifying. Upper Britain, despite its flourishing society, could not be seen to be too exciting, otherwise there would be revolt.

Working Britain, given their geographical location with no way out, were effectively prisoners, but there was no need to make them painfully aware of their social blinkers, especially at a sensitive time like this. And so, after he had had a shower, slicked back his hair and sprayed on some of the cologne his daughter had bought him for his birthday, the Prime Minister found himself putting on a white shirt, cravat, waistcoat and jacket with gold cufflinks, accompanied by a pair of cotton trousers and shoes that screamed "decadence". He looked like your average mill owner of the 1830s – posh, authoritarian, a little chubby, but above all *not to be questioned*. He had to confess, although the flamboyancy was a little ridiculous, he rather liked the look.

The turn of the key in the lock downstairs, followed by the quiet opening and closing of the front door, signalled to him that Roberts was here. Brushing the lint off his shoulders, he descended downstairs to find him wrinkling his nose in front of the hallway mirror.

"Morning, sir," Roberts offered. The Prime Minister didn't return the greeting. Usually, he and Roberts got on well – almost like friends – but today was already destined to be a bad day, and he wasn't in the chirpiest of moods. After a moment's awkward pause, in which Roberts realised he wasn't going to get a response, he rummaged in the file he was carrying and handed a sheet of paper to the Prime Minister. "Your itinerary for today, sir. We'll be using the Piccadilly entrance, as it's the most convenient, and then we'll proceed to the Buckingham slums, with an armed guard –"

"Thank you, Roberts, I can read," the PM muttered irritably, casting his eye over the day's plans. It was as he'd thought – Working Buckingham 6, followed by a visit to Mess Hall CQ in the Working South Bank, with a final journey over to the Working Wembley Amphitheatre to deliver his speech about the immigration lottery. He grimaced. Was this really so important that they had to send him? With a sigh that resonated through every cell in his body, the Prime Minster tucked the itinerary into his inside pocket and walked out of Number One Downing Street to the already-waiting car.

The streets were deserted, but the hum of the mazes below continued unabated, constant, no matter what time it was. Tourists on British soil would often comment upon it, only to find that the native British – having heard the same background drone since birth – had no idea what they were talking about. The workers were designated shifts so that the production lines and heavy machinery and coal mines and workshops and power stations and water towers were always manned, maintained and kept running. Filthy, impoverished and sickening the system may have been, but no-one could doubt Working Britain for its efficiency. As for those in Upper Britain, the country was – through its exclusive, special trade relationship with those downstairs – the most prosperous in the world. Hardly anyone in the Provinces got up before ten, and those who did, did so because they liked mornings (or had insomnia). Everything was so cheap that money in the UP was now more of a hobby than a means to live. Sustenance for a week could be purchased for pennies. The going rate was 1,046 US Dollars to the pound. Those who went abroad became the ultimate philanthropists. Indeed – a trend had begun only the previous month in South America of setting up tramps for life just by bringing over a couple of hundred to hand out. The media had coined the term "hobohols" for this type of excursion. The rest of the world had theme parks for fun – Upper Britain had just changed the focus from thrill-seeking to salving its collective ego.

As the car pulled into Piccadilly Circus, the Prime Minister glanced out of the tinted windows. Empty. Sure, it would become a nice little hub of activity come lunchtime, but for now there was no-one but him, his aides, two burly-looking security guards and a couple of chauffeurs.

Wait.

Blinking, he looked again. In the corner of his eye, he had spotted that something was amiss, but it was too subconscious, too vague to place. Eyebrows, narrowed, he stepped out of the now-stationary car and glanced around. No-one... but... there! Over on the other end of the square, between two roads, was a man behind a camera, crouched, with tousled hair and sunglasses. The Prime Minister started. There was a citywide ban on press photography of senior state officials. He went to call out, but as he did so, the two made eye contact.

Despite the hundred-yard gap between the two, he could see something strange in the man's eyes, something no-one really saw anymore, some echo of a former time. Fear? Apprehension? Was this man *scared*? But there was something else there altogether more alien, something he didn't recognise at all. At the last moment, before his cry took verbal form, he swallowed his exclamation and let the man be. There was something about this one that provoked a sense of curiosity in him, and he didn't want police tarnishing that mystery.

He needed a distraction in the meantime. "Roberts!" He clicked his fingers, and the aide scuttled over. "Get me a line of coke. I need something to pep me up before I go down there." Roberts bowed his head in silent admonition, walked briskly off to the car and returned with a tiny plastic test tube of the white stuff. He handed it to the Prime Minister, who popped the cap off and snorted it. He shuddered for a brief second, then whirled around to the now-open exit ramp, brimming with confidence. At the bottom, he could see the rush of vagrants behind the ceiling-high metal mesh fence, murmuring, growling, sounding more like beasts than people. His lip curled as he descended, led by two burly, Neanderthal men, armed with sub-automatic guns.

He and his companions reached the bottom, face to face with the citizens of Working London – people who were now cowering in the threat of weaponry. They entered a small room to the left, leaving the spectators behind, where a tired-looking border official was sat, leaning back on his chair and picking his nose. These rooms hadn't been done up since the fifties – the wallpaper was yellowing, and there were still filing cabinets in the room, presumably filled with records. Border official was about the shittiest job you could get, and the nonchalant state of the man behind the desk certainly backed this up.

This said, he beamed when they entered – citizens of Upper Britain rarely came to visit; this was a pleasant surprise. He and Roberts exchanged a few formalities, then he went over to the solid titanium door in the corner of the room, and punched in a series of numbers into the electronic keypad. There was a click and a series of low whirrs, and the door slowly opened, revealing the dark, wet entrance corridor, spiralling down, lit only by yellow, flickering lamps every ten yards or so. In a heightened state, the Prime Minister, cocaine lifting away any rose-tinted glasses he might have subconsciously been wearing, stepped forward nervously. He had been down through this entrance dozens of times, but it still gave him the willies. Especially the Buckingham slums – those, he hadn't been to in years. The reports had been saying that living standards had fallen, but he didn't really know what to expect. His shoes landed softly against the dusty, packed earth, beating a steady, echoing rhythm that plodded on at a quarter of the pace of his racing heartbeat. He realised that this sort of visit required a downer drug, something to dull the senses, but it was too late now. He took in a deep, self-conscious inhalation of the soil-tainted air, and carried on to the end of the tunnel.

Finally, the guards slowed to a stop and parted to let the Prime Minister past. The tunnel opened out to a rocky ridge that peered over Buckingham 6, with rough-hewn steps down to the bottom leading off to the right. The Prime Minister surveyed the slums below, and saw a nightmare.

It was a scene reminiscent of the outskirts of Mumbai. The slums extended for about eight miles, stopped only by a colossal factory in the distance, its chimneys jutting up through the ceiling to the surface. Once, these slums had been sparsely populated, vagrants scuttling from each corrugated iron shelter to the next, but now the sight that greeted the Prime Minister was one of utmost horror and dread. The shelters had been abandoned long ago, perhaps with the realisation that a roof already existed far above them. Thousands – hundreds of thousands of people lay strewn out on rags of cloth or just the bare earth, some dead, some still alive – for today, at least, and with no real distinction between the two. Below, the ant-like people continued to scuttle, but with less of that contained urgency that had charmed the Prime Minister years ago. The sheer degeneration in such a short time was incredible, terrifying.

The leader and figurehead of Upper Britain felt suddenly self-conscious. His heart was going like a double-speed clock – ticktickticktick... he tried to calm down, reassuring himself. *It's the drugs. Don't worry. It's all just the drugs.* But each glimpse back down at the massive-scale squalor sent him off again. Why had no-one informed him about such a huge change? Who in his Cabinet was responsible for keeping him in the dark? Hell – did even *they* know?

His eyes, bloodshot from exaggerated anxiety and suspicion, darted from aide to security guard to official to civil servant to every single person who had descended with him, all of them now standing on the ridge. Any one of them could have known about this mess. This was worse than any poverty he had ever seen. There were poor African children in the world, having to walk eighteen miles a day for fresh water, but those kids were living it up in comparison to the urchins of this hellish underworld.

He could hear his temples throbbing that same suspense-filled heartbeat, a deafening roar that nearly drowned out Roberts, who was by now standing directly next to him. "I said, shall we proceed down, sir?" For a second, he remained dazed, then seemed to sense the gist of Roberts' question and whirled his head round, sweat and fear running down his face, mingling with tears of absolute overwhelming terror. He opened his mouth, but no sound came out. Finally, a croak surfaced from his throat.

"No. I... I mean... I can't... I... n-no -"

And with that, he darted back up the tunnel, leaving everyone assembled perplexed.

Surfacing into the air, air that he gulped down in greedy mouthfuls, his head slowly but surely stopped spinning. The vein on his forehead that previously stood out like a bolt of lightning now receded, leaving just a sheen of sweat that reflected the sun. Now, the drugs were wearing off, and he was glad – where he'd thought that he'd need it to take away the boredom, he had really needed something to mellow his spirit, to make him not give a damn.

Of course, the Prime Minister wasn't a moralist. He couldn't be, not in the position he held. But there was a scale. There was the exploitation of an underclass of citizens, and then there was out-and-out slavery unparalleled since the years before the Abolitionist movement. Before, they had been slums with character – the odd smiling face here and there, a general optimism prevailing over the tough times – but here... whatever flicker of conscience in the Prime Minister there still was, it was suddenly aflame, tearing through his gut. It was the sheer *scale* of it – rows upon rows of people hemmed in like animals. They were meant to be workers, not the product of some factory-farming scheme.

He looked around. By himself, the strange photographer nowhere to be seen, he was completely alone in Piccadilly Circus. The sun hung precariously low in the sky, not yet complete in its ascent. He walked, slowly and surely so as not to disturb the quiet, over to the steps of a nearby building, and sat down. He mopped his drenched brow with his sleeve, and looked out on the mist and the red dawn. Was the suffering below worth it for this beauty? He had to admit, anywhere you went in London was perfect, and the millions below would ruin it in an instant, but was it worth the suffering?

He shivered – not from the cold, but from the dangerous shift in ideology he found himself experiencing. In the space of thirty minutes or so, he had gone from a callous, mean-hearted capitalist, to a... not a *humanitarian*, but something with more of a moral standing than before. Perhaps the reform he had suggested was still a little too harsh. Maybe it was time for a bigger compromise...

With a short, sharp cough, Roberts re-appeared from the exit ramp, glancing around. It was only here that the Prime Minister realised he had been crying. Drying his eyes hastily, he got up and walked over, sniffing, trying to keep a stiff upper lip. He came to a stop in front of his aide, who was distinctly out of breath – he had run back. Perhaps he understood. The PM ventured a forlorn smile, which Roberts returned. For a moment, it looked as if he was about to reach out and touch his superior's arm – no amorous intent, just friendly reassurance – but at the last minute he withdrew, instead bowing his head hesitantly.

Perhaps it was the fact that he knew someone who understood, but this exchange caused the PM to choke back more tears, trying as much as he could to stay strong but failing.

He heard the sound of the other Cabinet ministers and the security guards coming back up, and hastily got into the car. He could trust in Roberts, but the Cabinet were a bunch of backstabbing, conniving men and women who always looked out for a sign of weakness in their peers, hoping to exploit it for their own gain. He would recover in the trip over, but for now he wanted to be invisible.

As they drove to the next location, a singular line of black cars on the empty London streets, he reassured himself. At least with the next stop, he wouldn't have to worry about scale. For each community, there were about 500 mess halls, each about the size of a smallish hall – a little smaller than the main chamber of Parliament. True, at feeding times the rooms would be packed to capacity, but it was easier to deal with from a spectator's point of view.

Now resolved and calmed down, his thoughts returned to the mystery photographer and that look that was so alien. He accepted that the man was scared, and this was fair enough – he had, after all, been caught in the act by the most senior politician nationwide. But there was still that other *something* at the back of his mind, the emotion he couldn't quite place, niggling away, refusing to be ignored. It annoyed him, and it was perhaps this that made him step out of the car in just as foul a mood as he had been in when he had woken up. This time, though, he softened his tone to Roberts, who now felt almost like an estranged younger brother – consciously and publicly, they were as distant as any two professionals, but there was a warmer undercurrent of mutual understanding.

As the guards unlocked the cover that lay over the controls for the underground lift, Roberts handed the Prime Minister a pair of earmuffs. He wrinkled his nose in confusion and mild disgust – they were, after all, *furry*. Sensing this, Roberts explained.

"It can get pretty loud down there. It's not exactly necessary, but you might find it a lot less comfortable if you don't wear them." Resigned, the PM put them on. He already looked like a prat; what was the point in arguing now?

Through the protective material, he heard the hum of the elevator as it approached the surface. It got louder and louder, until the titanium-reinforced concrete floor panels slid apart and the lift rose the last few feet, slowly and surely, to the street level. It was a completely glass structure, reminiscent of some fantasy creation by one of his favourite childhood authors; that said, it served the practical purpose of note being spotted by those approaching from far off. Doubtless, people knew of the lifts' existence (there was usually at least one in each community), but it was never going to get the public into a frenzy of admiration and excitement.

The doors opened, and he and Roberts stepped in. Again, his question was sensed by the aide, when the rest of the party didn't step in. He lifted his earmuffs off temporarily, to allow Roberts to speak.

"We felt that if you were in a large group, you might feel a little less... yourself." Was he being patronised, or did Roberts genuinely care? Either way, as the security guards took a square formation around the lift and they began to descend, it was probably irrelevant.

For a split second as the slabs slid over above them, he and Roberts were plunged into total darkness, broken only when the lights – dirty yellow and flickering, around since the birth of electricity – came on down the sides of the earthen elevator shaft. He felt a little claustrophobic – not panicking, thankfully, but aware that he was, essentially, in a box being lowered by a string. Nausea trickled around his stomach, softly purring, threatening to burn into a hiss but never going too far. When the doors opened and they stepped into the bare entrance area, the dirty air was a welcome relief – it felt more suitable than the stale, carbon dioxide-filled interior of the glass booth behind him.

They were now facing down a seemingly endless corridor that curved round at the end, with a pair of ornate wooden doors on either side every twenty feet or so. Each one led out into a mess hall, and had a number crudely daubed on in white paint. Although on a mechanical level every mess hall was the same, each series – the Working South Bank, Working Buckingham, Working Camden – had been designed by a different architect when the Working Britain Aid Fund was introduced in 1938.

Their current location, Working Kensington, was easily the nicest – rather than pools, each hall was split into nine troughs – there was even seating at one point, though that had been stolen away by the workers. He straightened his top hat, breathed deeply in through his nose, and strode through the doors.

Even through his earmuffs, the first thing that hit him was the noise; shattering, ear-bleeding pandemonium that bounced off the walls, creating a thoroughly disorientating experience. People of all ages jostled to get to the troughs, unaware of and with complete disregard to the fact that they were being watched. One thing that could be said for these people was their sense of relative equality – women and children were not granted any special privileges, and hence had to be twice as insistent to get to the front. Despite this desperate crush of people, there was nothing yet in the troughs, which looked as if they had been licked clean.

The mess halls were a government initiative, and had come about a long time after the first Segregation Orders of 1798 and 1803. After a hundred or so years of Working Britain's existence, famine had crept in. Some foodstuffs could be produced underground, but not enough, and this essentially meant workers were dying off. In turn, this meant a loss of fuel and resources, and even more importantly, a loss of saleable products for Upper Britain to sell. An initiative that was once intended to restore peace and order to those above the ground was now crippling them, and it was at this point that the mess halls were introduced.

The food was awful – a swill that was comparable to pig food, only worse. But it was packed in nutrients conducive to productivity – carbohydrates and proteins were top of the list – and more importantly, it was cheap. What's more, to outside nations, it seemed like a benevolent gesture; a country suffering from abject poverty was being provided with constant sustenance, something that the entire world still hadn't managed to do for countries like Uganda and Mozambique.

The machines ground into life, and like some sort of open plumbing system the liquid nutrition gushed down each pipe, thick and sludge-like, stinking to high heaven. The Prime Minister flinched as the crowds – previously just noisy – turned feral, surging forwards. They were like animals; Roberts, who had retreated to take a surreptitious call, shadowed from the masses, had to shout above the din, and even then he was barely audible. People were trampled, bloodied and weak under the feet of the starving hundreds. Those at the front greedily scooped the muck into their mouths with filthy hands, stopping only when they lost focus and were pushed aside by others. Here, thank God, was an example of how times hadn't changed – the lower classes were just as bad – not worse, in fairness, but no better either – as before.

Seeing this constancy allowed the PM to relax a little, but only until a piece of carrot covered in the glutinous brown gunk flew up and hit him on the cheek. It didn't look deliberate, more some frantic flailing gesture gone wrong – but he could see the culprit leering at him, presumably trying to strike an "aw, shucks" stance. Grimacing, he wiped it away, beckoning to Roberts, never taking his eyes off the assailant. Roberts, having finished his call and now noticeably anxious, drew up beside him.

"Roberts? Do you see that man?" The aide's eyeline drew to meet that of the PM's. He nodded.

"Yes, sir."

"See to it that he's executed, would you?" he requested tersely, allowing himself a glimmer of grim satisfaction – his cynicism, his old self, was returning. This was good – in a job such as his, it didn't do well to be too caring – and after all, why *should* he care? Looking down at these ravenous, ugly people, it was clear they had become something... inhuman, some subspecies, an offshoot of the human race that had somehow devolved.

He noticed that Roberts was still anxious. Either he needed the loo, or something was up. "What is it?" he snapped, and Roberts began to speak like an uncorked champagne bottle – his words, uncontrolled, frothed over, bumbling in desperate urgency.

"Aha... um... there's been a change of plan, sir. It appears that in the amphitheatre in Working Wembley, a riot's broken out – a couple of fathers got into an argument or something, and it just escalated. The place is a red zone, sir – no citizen of Upper Britain is allowed underground there for the next 48 hours." The PM's shoulders slumped. This whole rigmarole had all been for nothing? "So instead, they want you to do the speech here." The Prime Minister blinked, speechless. "We'll still have a digital relay running. You won't cover the whole of London, I'm afraid, but it'll suffice. Is it

OK if I..." Roberts tentatively attached a radio microphone to the Prime Minister's lapel; stunned that he was about to conduct a historic speech in such a depressing hovel of a place, the Prime Minister didn't move, allowing himself to be wired up.

The mob had had their fill, and now milled about distracted, waiting for the sirens to ring to send them back to work. Twitching bodies with various injuries littered the floor, disregarded by the workers, whose eyes just seemed dead. No sirens came, and instead there was the sound of a nervous man clearing his throat, followed by the sharp, puffed-up intake of breath from the Prime Minister. To the PM's dismay, the suspense and excitement he was trying to create had gone ignored, with the odd citizen casually glancing upward disinterestedly. He went on, regardless:

"People of Working London, I stand before you on this... momentous day to announce something to you. What happens today is the product of years of negotiation, of deliberation, of compromise. This new development between our two proud nations could benefit any one of you."

At the word "benefit", a few more ears pricked up, and a few more people turned around, but it was hardly impressive. God knows what those in the other mess halls must be doing – he almost felt glad that he couldn't see the vast majority of the people he was talking to. Picking at their filthy nails, probably, still waiting for the siren. He began to feel uncomfortable, but then he felt a flood of calm wash over him from somewhere. But where? He looked around the unsanitary subterranean canteen, and found his solace in the face of a small, 12 or 13-year-old boy. His eyes – huge, after years of environmental adaptation in an underground environment – shone with passionate attention, much unlike everyone else, who at best managed a lazy stare. It was a mixture of love and fascination, but more importantly of hope. That anyone in this hovel could actually have aspirations brought a lump to the minister's throat, and he knew that this boy, regardless of anything in the approved plans of a citywide lottery, was going to be chosen. Making sure that no-one was looking but the boy – they weren't –

66

he quickly pulled out his cameraphone and took a snapshot, then returned to his speech with the air of someone delivering a pointless lecture to a disinterested group of students.

"One of you," he said, looking directly at the boy, "is to be selected to be granted full citizenship of Upper Britain." Silence. These people didn't give a damn. They'd spent years in thrall of the world above, only to find that it didn't provide anything but pig swill and hard labour. Who could want a world that only produces that? "Y-you will be provided with a full education, luxurious living, and -" Still faced, with no reaction, he turned to Roberts. "This is a waste of time. They don't give a shit." And, red-faced and humiliated, he stormed out, every one of the brainless drones not even batting an eyelid.

Nearly everyone.

*

[a week later]

From outside the Prime Minister's office, there came three timid knocks. Finishing a handwritten note to his PA – asking her to nip and out and buy some more coffee – he set his pen down and let out a contented sigh. This was it. Anticipation shivered through him. He coughed, injected a little confidence into his demeanour.

"Come in," he said. The doors opened, and there –

It was if he was observing a docile, newborn child. Those eyes, suddenly alien in this new world, roved the room, taking in every detail, wild, greedily swallowing up every visual stimulus. The same eyes eventually came to a stop on the Prime Minister.

Frozen in that moment, there was a simple exchange of glances, where all the complex political problems, all those ethical dilemmas, the same stress that had lost the minister so much sleep just evaporated. Everything felt a little simpler. He was a man, faced with a boy, and he was going to help the boy out.

Chapter Three

On the fifth of May two thousand and six, Daniel Rassetter falls in love with a moon-eyed boy called Paul, Paul Lincoln, one of those perfect men who are simultaneously ruggedly handsome and have the sort of eyes that let you glimpse their soul in its rawest form. Daniel is nineteen years of age, and he and Paul have only just met, but Daniel knows that right now, in this instant, they have to make love. Of course, they're in a classroom, one full of students, so he might have to compromise, but he knows it's just a matter of waiting.

It's a strange time to be gay. To live as a teenager in the twenty-first century is very different to living as an adult. Adults dictate the laws, and the laws still say that homosexuality's illegal, punishable by either chemical castration or twenty years in prison. But the adults also know that it's one of those stupid laws that are unenforceable, like copyright, because everyone's doing it. In the year two thousand and six, everyone does everyone, and doesn't make any bones about it – not a second for the law, people just laugh. Daniel Rassetter, though, he's a bit of a loner, bit of a romantic, still believes in those dreamy sunset notions like "The One" and "monosexualism" – sure he's had sex with girls and guys, but he never really liked the girls and the guys never understood him, they were just looking for a cheap ride.

Paul Lincoln, though, he senses in Paul that there's something different about him, and spends a whole hour in his lecture just wanting to kiss him. That poor lecturer (Thom Kilburn, PhD.) could have explained a perfect way to end world hunger, and Daniel would be none the wiser, because his eyes are focused on the back of Paul's head, imagining his attentive expression, wanting to stare into the lakes of his eyes.

When time's called, he dashes to the door and waits, waits, waits for Paul to emerge. He doesn't, not even when everyone in the lecture theatre's left, so he nervously walks back in, on tenterhooks in case the lecturer's still there, having a quick fuck session with some office tart, but no – it's empty, save for Paul in the centre, scribbling down notes, in the middle of his own ghost lesson. The determination in Paul's eyes, that expression, it makes Daniel melt inside, and he has to lean on the table just to stay upright.

The table moves an inch. It scrapes on the floor.

Paul looks up.

Instantly, as their eyes meet, Daniel feels a connection, and bounds up the steps, running down the aisle, and bowling Paul over. Paul laughs, and the two kiss ferociously. Daniel realises in a second that Paul's perfect – there's a sense of damaged innocence he's been looking for all his life, something he so wanted for himself but grew up in an environment that spat on individualism and made you learn so fast. They cling to each other as if the second they split a gaping chasm'll open up between them, lava firing up sending heat mirages that forever obscure this perfect view, a desperation that is both perfectly timed and imperfectly so – even in this place, students aren't allowed in the lecture theatres outside hours.

Paul pulls away, stares at Daniel so the two can see their reflections in each other's eyes, whispers "tonight", then gets up and runs off, laughing silently to himself. Daniel's left exhilarated, panting, smiling in a glow he hasn't felt since his age only stretched to single figures.

*

Two months later, Daniel's sitting on the bedroom floor of Paul's room. Paul's on the bed. Daniel wants to be on the bed too, but Paul asked him to sit down when he came in, not even exchanging a glance. Daniel's cheeks are still flushed, and neither of them have done anything yet – but this feels odd.

Two months, the two have been meeting for regular fuck sessions. Daniel's loved it. He hasn't felt about anyone like this before. He sees Paul, and right away his eyes go out of focus, his lip trembles and all the air rushes out of his body. That's what he takes to be love – the fact that Paul can produce such an immense physical reaction in him. To Daniel, it *is* love.

Paul sighs, lying there, perfect and vulnerable, yet commanding some sort of authority in his elevated position. A couple of times he stops and starts, nearly saying something but not, and it's clear that he wants to say something but doesn't know how. Daniel's about to talk, when Paul finally speaks.

"I'm tired."

You can hear the cars going past outside. Daniel smiles.

"What're you tired of?"

More cars, the rustling of trees, the animated chatter of other people down the corridor that Paul lives on.

"I expected more... I don't know. It's hard to explain. What we do – not just us, everyone our age – it just doesn't feel right. We just hop onto every passing dick, never really thinking if we suit each other, all just to satisfy our own urges... it just feels strange."

Daniel narrows his eyebrows. He thought they were different. Two months is a long time for a relationship. Most burn out after a few days, and the more lasting ones still end after a month or so. He thought he was showing commitment. Love. Passion. Everything you could want in a boyfriend.

Paul sits up, twists his body round to face Daniel, and crosses his legs. He's wearing a cerulean hoodie, and a pair of jeans, worn around the ankles. No socks. Daniel doesn't think he's ever seen Paul wearing socks. Paul stares down at Daniel.

"We call it love, sure, but is it? Do we ever actually think about it? Can you honestly say you've reflected once on your own feelings and seen if we suit each other at all? Aren't we supposed to think about the people we love?"

Daniel's disturbed by all of this. Theirs has been a relationship defined by long, blissful silences and spine-tingling action in the bedroom, not long and meaningful conversations. He's not sure if he likes the way Paul's speaking. For a second or two, he considers getting up and walking out, feeling that he should have some sort of reaction to what Paul's saying, but can't muster up the motivation. He stays sitting, staring back at Paul, waiting for him to go on.

Paul wants a response, but doesn't get one, so he elaborates. "When you imagine me, do you ever get beyond what I look like, or are there any personal qualities that you like about me?"

Daniel dips his head, thinks. Brings his head back up again, smiles, and says quietly, "I like the way you speak. I like your voice." Paul blinks. He knows that Daniel's missed the point, and it terrifies him. Daniel's the most passionate person he's ever met, and even he doesn't get the thoughts that have been plaguing him since he came up from below. His entire adolescent life's been lived out up here, but now that he feels the raging hormones of puberty ebbing away, he's left with a lot of unanswered questions coming from underground, questions no-one else seems interested in answering.

Paul tries to remember his old family. They don't feel like family anymore, but he can remember his biological father trying to give what underground they called "the Talk" – a brief, awkward description of sex, and what it meant. Only people who truly love each other should have sex, his Dad had said. Only if you truly care about them, and you can see yourself sharing your life with them. He remembers his Dad laughing here, nudging Paul's ten-year-old self and saying under his breath that it's fine to find them attractive too, smiling and looking over to Paul's mother.

That just seems alien, now – the only part remaining is the physical attraction, and he *is* attracted to Daniel – he has a sort-of movie star look, physically looking older than his years. Inside, though, Paul feels that Daniel, Gail, Teresa, Harold, Sasha, every sexual partner he's ever had – they're just children, on the inside, fucking against the backdrop of a world that can't be bothered to preserve some sense of interpersonal connection.

In most respects, Paul's glad that he can't remember much of his life before he turned thirteen and was yanked out from the ground, uprooted for no reason other than his fascination with the Prime Minister, a man who wore such strange but enchanting clothes. Of course, he learnt that even that was a sham, put on to satisfy the querulous attitude of the older people with inherited memories – all the stories of the World Above had been fabricated from stories hundreds of years old.

Upper Britain... it delighted and depressed him. The one reason he didn't try and expose Working Britain to the truth was fear – not fear that he'd be thrown into the public eye, but fear that he might lose this wonderful new world. But there were parts that just didn't fit – he was growing up in a generation of people who seemed totally isolated – oblivious to the world below them, and to their parents and grandparents. There was the stench of nihilism everywhere – sometimes, it was freeing, but all too often it did nothing but make Paul feel alone.

Quietly, Paul asks Daniel to leave, and tells him that he doesn't want to see him for a while. It's a lie. Paul doesn't want to see Daniel ever again, but people like Daniel still cling onto the romance in old movies, reusing those lines without understanding the subconscious ideas behind them – if Paul says "I never want to see you again", Daniel will respond with a fit of tears and something like "you never cared for me", when Daniel doesn't understand for a moment what caring means – that's not to say that he doesn't care, somewhere buried in his inaccessible thoughts, but that he's never really thought about what caring *means*.

As Daniel leaves, Paul starts to cry a little. With Daniel, he felt that he had found someone who was compatible at last, someone who was going through the same process. But it had ended up with a similar result. Daniel differs from the others in that he at least feels a degree of emotion, but his approach to it is childish, undeveloped, ignorant. Perhaps he'll learn as time goes by, but with no instruction from above or within, how can he?

Perhaps he's destined to be alone, Paul thinks. Perhaps that's the sacrifice one makes in living above ground – in enjoying a beautiful world, full of light and fields and vast, blue oceans, free of the dirt in his old life, he has to accept that this life is one free of personal connection.

Daniel walks away, shocked and upset, but he can't for a moment understand why. He's had tens, hundreds of relationships since he entered his teens, but they've never ended like this before. He feels like a neutered lion, desperate to roar with rage but each bellow caught in his throat before he can let it loose. It's totally alien to him, and it scares him. When he gets home, he paces the room, trying to recover from the shock, and for the first time in his life an introspective curiosity floods his body. And as he thinks, he realises that the approach he's developing, of thinking about what it means to love, probably came too late.

Chapter Four

It had been a cloak-and-dagger affair, something I was fairly accustomed to. From an untraceable email address, I'd been asked to find out who killed Paul Lincoln, and promised a reward of £10,000 if I managed it. Once upon a time, that meant someone really cared, but in the last few decades the police had gone from being conscientious people with a lot of time on their hands, to a bunch of alcoholic cynics, finally realising that in a crime-free Britain, the police are a redundant asset. They'd lost their touch, but they were more than happy to hire out others to do their work for them. And a government budget goes a long way.

I also had the advantage of being strictly off-the-record. I could go places that the government couldn't, use methods that were strictly illegal. It's for that reason that I was good at what I did. Sure, I might have bugged a few phones and broken a few fingers in my time, but I'd only ever lost one case. I was seen to be good at the job, and that's why they'd already shipped out the initial payment of five grand, putting it down on their claims forms as ten new computers.

Lincoln was interesting. Killed two months ago in a back alley. Any murder was unheard of, but one that was apparently calculated was even rarer. Murderers in Upper Britain were usually insane, and killed with no real discretion or respect for keeping out of jail. In that respect, it was strange. In all others, not so much.

No-one knows this apart from the people that matter (and me), but Lincoln was from the underground. I know. I never expected it – I since learned that he was the first in a governmental experiment to see how the lower classes functioned above ground. I'd hacked into the computer of his psychoanalyst, and discovered twenty-odd years of files that indicated that he hadn't been too well. Paul was a man who'd been fed stories about heroism and beauty against all the odds at an early age, formative views that just don't work up here. His entire adolescent life had been a mess, as he continually attempted to integrate himself and failed miserably, and while it had improved once he graduated from university – as a lawyer, he'd managed to live out his childhood fantasies of helping people out, to an extent – the lawyers were just as short of real work as the police were. Apparently, he'd almost considered suicide for a while, during one of his dry spells at work. But... no – it didn't fit, especially when I considered that he'd just won the biggest case of his life on the day he was shot.

This brought it down to three options, none of which were particularly convincing:

1. *Right-wing extremists.* I hoped it wasn't this, just because if it was political then it was probably given to a hitman, and they were impossible to track down. Sadly, this was also the most convincing of the three, given Lincoln's background as a child of the underground, and getting into the Prime

Minister's records wasn't too hard. If I could do it, the crazies probably could too.

2. *Someone connected to the Lündstrom case.* Peter Lündstrom had gone through an episode on cocaine where he raped his own wife and killed her brother, and Lincoln was responsible for putting him in jail. Lündstrom was also a fairly sociable guy, so it was quite possible that someone who felt close to him had gone out on a rampage. But that was unlikely – I'd investigated his close friends, and there seemed to be no-one with any interest right to the point in killing his jailer, but it wasn't quite closed yet.

3. *An insanity case.* The least likely of the three, because of what I've already mentioned. Whoever this was, it was a calculated attack, not one done on a whim or based off paranoia or anger.

Today was going to be fairly exciting, though – in a fairly bizarre move, given it was meant to be a standard police job, the first thing I'd done was go to the murder scene (still with blood on the floor) and take swabs of everything I could see. It had been a back alley near Lincoln's home, fairly overgrown and without any trace of people frequenting it, so I took swabs of everything I could see and – this is the funny part – sent it off to Scotland Yard with a quick backhander. That's right – the police paid me illegally so I could persuade another division of the police to act illegally. Fucking poetic. Either way, today was the day I was getting the results back.

It arrived by special delivery at 11:05am, on a USB stick. I'd been hoping for handwritten notes, but it was mechanically cold – if we were going by fingerprints and sweat analysis, there were five potentials. One was Lincoln himself, and I was sure it wasn't him alone. The next were a couple, Michael and Sarah Portman, a married couple who lived two doors up. I doubted it was them, but scribbled them down. Another was Paul's next-door-neighbour, Samuel Gardiner, an Alabaman who ran his own cannabis store near my flat. Another unlikely suspect, given his predisposition to hugging me every time I walked into the shop. In fact, there was only one who stood out as potentially alien – a 35-year-old male from Leeds, name David Sullivan, with no profession registered, but that didn't matter – I already knew who he was. We'd met before.

*

"Who put you up to it this time?"

There he was. David Sullivan. One of the most prolific hitmen in the country. If I was the private detective you came to if you wanted the job done, he was the hitman. He was my one lost case – a perfect crime, connected only by a name that his contractors wouldn't testify to. David was so good, he could shoot a man in a courtroom and still leave no trace. Why I'd manage to find him was anyone's guess. Perhaps I was close to the truth all along – perhaps he'd gone nuts.

We were in a coffee shop – he was sitting there, casually munching on a Danish pastry, I was standing above him. He motioned for me to take a seat, and I accepted. Even now, I was amazed at his nonchalance – everyone knew what he did, but he just didn't care. At my question, he smiled at me.

"No hello? No hug for old time's sake? You're a very impolite man, Terence." I stared at him. Here I was, in possession of information that could land him a life sentence, and he was just sitting there criticising my sense of propriety. "First off, let's settle the usual. My guess is that the government will have offered you about £15,000 to get me. I want to give you ten times that sum." I blinked. "Come on, the amount of corporate customers I've had... the amount of money I've got, I can afford to let a little go here and there."

Sullivan knew how the police force worked. He knew that with any murder investigation even verging on high-profile, they'd send me out. And I could be bribed. If the police were the knights on white horses, their steeds locked up in the stables for an indefinitely long winter, I was their farmhand – a well-paid farmhand, in fairness, but one that would run off in a minute if he was paid any more. Sure, I might be in the employ of an assassin, but oddly enough that wasn't something I felt uncomfortable with. I smiled grimly. He'd won.

He'd known that I'd spent years wanting to catch him, but that it was more a case of satisfying my own curiosity than getting justice for his victims. Now he'd laid out a perfectly solvable crime, but he knew he could pay me not to tell. And if I did? Well, let's say that Sullivan's as good at his job as I am at mine. And that's good.

"The look on your face."

I paused, then nodded. "Alright."

He took another bite of his Danish pastry, still looking at me. I could tell that he was waiting for me to ask questions, and I didn't want to humour him – I knew he wouldn't answer. For a few moments, all that could be heard was the sound of a baby crying in the corner, the smooth jazz coming from the speakers and the low murmur of a half-dozen conversations.

I closed my eyes. "Answers, though. This one just lost me. Who put you up to it this time?" He laughed.

"Tell you what, I'll give you three options."

"I already had three options – turns out I was wrong." He paused and looked at me, apparently concerned. After a moment or two, he shook himself out and returned to his smiling self.

"OK – first one – the right-wing extremists put me up to it." I looked at him, rolling my eyes.

"You know I know it wasn't them. They couldn't afford you."

"I know – I was testing you. There's signs that you're losing your touch, Terence -" (I hated being called Terence) "- and I couldn't possibly have that. You make things exciting. Alright then, here's the real options."

He took another bite, put the pastry down, and laid his hands out in front of him.

"The government paid me to do it, or no-one did."

I paused, and leaned back on the chair, thinking. Government corruption was more plausible, even if it did have a sick poetry to it – pay for the murder and the investigation. "Why would the government pay you?"

He sighed. "Their little experiment hadn't worked. Think about it – this was meant to be their first attempt at integrating the Underground, and if you look at his psych profile – as I'm sure you have – it wasn't exactly working. Sure, he was an OK lawyer, but it was his morals driving him, and because of that he got on the tits of everyone he worked with. Either he was happy and making everyone else miserable, or the world carried on by without giving him a second glance. Or, for that matter, a first. Not exactly a success story, is it?"

I drummed my fingers on the table. "No reason to kill him, though."

"Are you serious? OK, granted, *I'm* expensive, but the amount it was costing to track *him*... he had his own private psychoanalyst, doctor, a health insurance plan that covered bills up to twenty-five million, not to mention the 24-hour surveillance team that I had to bypass. It was costing them over a *million* each year just to allow him to stay above ground."

I nodded. He had a point. It was miserable, reducing it to finance, but it made sense. There was, of course, the other option, which didn't.

"Why would you kill him? I can't see you doing it just for kicks."

This produced a longer pause from him, and my pensive expression was for a moment mirrored.

"I've been thinking. Over the years, I've built up a fairly extensive network of people who owe me favours. I've basically got the means to stage a revolution. All it took was a dead body, and me giving the orders." Seeing my blank expression, he carried on. "Have you seen a picture of the guy? Undergrounder from a mile off – you can tell from the eyes and the complexion, and Working Britain know their own kind. I know the coroner in the morgue where he was being kept, and someone who works in aid deliveries to down below – bedding, that sort of thing. If I could get his body down there, make them see what the world above their heads does to their kind, then we'd see unprecedented anger, and sooner or later there'd be a massive uprising. It'd be the end of this country!" He leaned back, laughing, bordering on hysterical. I was staring.

It was a good minute or so before he stopped, and looked back at me. "So. What do you think?"

"Why would you want a revolution?"

He looked through me, speaking to no-one, but I listened anyway.

"I'm bored, Terence... we say we're living in a perfect country, leader of the free world and all that, but it's just... dull. We haven't had a political shake-up in over 200 years. We don't start or join wars anymore, because we've got a massively unfair advantage. Everything's great, sure, but we don't realise it because *there's nothing to contrast it against*. When was the last time you saw someone crying?"

"You want to make people cry?" His focus shifted back to me, shaking his head and looking disapproving.

"You're being deliberately dense."

It was true. I was. Perhaps I wanted to avoid what he was saying, but he was right – Upper Britain was a country of the living dead, people punching in and punching out. They played golf not because they liked the sport, but because it filled the hours. Hiked not for the scenery, but because it developed their muscles for all that nonexistent hard labour. Bought the latest 3D televisions and tablet PCs because they were there, not because they really wanted them.

Maybe we needed a shake-up. It was a terrifying prospect, and maybe David Sullivan was a little mad in dreaming it up, but that didn't necessarily mean he was wrong....

David was busy putting his coat on. He finished off his Danish pastry, and gave me one last glance.

"Try and remember that the government theory has a lot more credibility." For another moment, he was lost in his own thoughts, raising his eyebrows at the ceiling. "And it suits me more, come to think of it."

And with that, he was gone.

Automobile

I woke up in the desert, and there was a dead giraffe on the back seat of my car. I had killed the giraffe some weeks back, on a trip out into the savannah, when the nukes hit and everything but me and my car was destroyed. At least, I assumed so. If it hadn't been for my emergency supplies, I would have been dead by now, and I was about to run out of petrol after a good five hundred miles of driving. The vultures were soaring overhead – or were they? I'd been rationing the water, and maybe the dehydration was causing hallucinations. They felt real.

I pulled up to a stop, and got out of the car to stretch my legs. The hot African sun beat down on my back as I stretched my legs and walked round to the other side of the car so I could open the door to the back seat – the heat, or the bombs, or maybe just time had welded the other door shut. The door, rusted and off-white, creaked as it opened, and there it was – flies buzzing away at it, red raw, the hair matted by now. I had no idea why I hadn't got rid of it yet. It was stinking out the car. But then, I guess I was going to have to abandon the car sooner or later and walk, and lugging the beast out of the vehicle could have dispensed with energy that I'd need later on.

As I started to back out of the car, someone tapped me on the back. In my haste to turn around, my head collided with the door of the car and I blacked out.

"Hey."

"What?"

"I think I've found it."

"It's supposed to be black, with a blue dot at the centre."

"Black... blue dot... yep."

I rubbed my eyes. I was lying on the ground, dust on my back, and there was a wet patch on the back of my head where I'd slammed it into the car door. It stang.

I sat up.

In front of me, three men were digging through the corpse of the giraffe. One was wearing a white robe and looked like Jesus with Death's face, another was half-naked and had an orange piece of cloth around his waist. The skin on his back was facing me, and it was peeling off in huge clumps, revealing darker pigments below. The other man seemed to be leading them, and was clad in a white T-shirt, waistcoat, cargo pants and a monocle. Around his waist was an adapted utility belt, filled with weaponry of various sorts – a shotgun on either side, a handgun, a couple of grenades, and so on. He seemed threatening – maybe it was just the way he was leaning against the shopping cart, a little defensively despite the fact that all it contained was junk from old computers, but he freaked me out a little. All of their hands were covered in blood.

"What are you doing?" The flies were deafening by now, drawn to the new flesh on display. They jumped back, startled. One of them was holding a small black box with a barely-perceptible navy blue dot in the centre. It too was covered in blood, and it looked like they'd grabbed it from the belly of the giraffe.

Once their alarm had been registered, they looked back down again and started wiping the blood off the box, as their apparent leader stepped forward towards me, casting his long shadow past me. It was getting late. The nights here were freezing, and I wondered how the other two would survive wearing so little.

The leader grabbed me by the scruff of the neck, hauled me upright and threw me against the car. My head was still bleeding from before, and I could feel my back bruising. He glared at me through his monocle, removed it and barked at me.

"WHO ARE YOU?"

I could hear myself whimpering, but couldn't quite believe it. He continued. "WHAT WERE YOU DOING WITH THAT ANIMAL?"

I opened my mouth to speak but nothing but air came out. He stood back for a second, staring at me, weighing me up. I wanted to run. God, I wanted to run. But as long as he was watching....

There was a clatter as the box hit the bottom of the shopping cart, and the leader suddenly whirled around towards the source of the noise. This was my chance. My legs suddenly came alive, I made to run off, a bullet hit me in the back of the head and for a gut-wrenching moment I realised that I'd become a peripheral character in someone else's narrative.

Bubbles

Summers were the worst.

I began the day by leaning over the side of my bunk, hacking up a piece of phlegm so big, it was a wonder it managed to escape from my throat. My fault. Smoker's cough. I didn't know of anyone here who didn't smoke. Everyone needs their own addiction, especially in a place like this.

We were the neglected. Over the hill, they were living it up as usual – sure, around September they'd start working, but even that was a breeze compared to us. Kids only expect Christmas presents once a year, but the little fuckers blow bubbles all the time.

I moved to Lapland for a change of scenery. The big city's all well and good, but y'know – it's nice to get out in the open once in a while, isn't it? That's what I thought at the time – get a one-way ticket, get a nice job ploughing snow or running tours around the area, and when I got bored I'd have the money to go home. Instead, I'm stuck in the only factory in the area that doesn't have any discrimination in their employment policies. Work in Christmas, you gotta be under four feet. Rainbow sherbet, which for some godforsaken reason is a booming industry round these parts, it's women-only. A 5'11" male from the Austin suburbs had no chance.

Factory floor. This is where we do the same mindless task day after day, no paid holidays, no medical, and don't even think about dental. Barney and I work on raw materials, the dirtiest and dullest job of the lot. We create the mix. Down the line, the bubbles are moulded, sent on and teleported to whichever delusional kid blows the next one. The job hasn't even got any rhythm – you have to go based on time zones. When you get to the time when East Africa's at midday, then we usually get a bit of break, but aside from that it's constant work. You'd think they'd make it so one global operation wasn't done from a single place. Then we wouldn't be forced into night shifts. And when I say "shift", we're talking twelve hours. Yeah. It's a 24-hour rotation system that just kills.

Why don't I go home? Two reasons. One, I can't. It's a slave wage here, because they know that if we're there, we don't have a choice. I barely have enough to live by, so getting a plane out of here is ridiculous to even think about. Two, in addition to being the only employment around here, I was also shoehorned into a three-year contract. Legally, I can't ship out until the end of 2011. And third, I don't want to risk it.

That last one requires a bit of explanation. Over time, a job like this turns you psychotic. These working conditions... we barely get to sleep, you've got about a fifty-fifty chance of contracting a fatal disease during your time on the floor, and there's never any leeway. If your kid suffers from the delusion that they can blow a bubble and it pops as soon as it reaches the air, that's not because we couldn't be bothered. We still spent time crafting that thing, but the teleport machine we're using dates back to the prehistoric ages, and doesn't always work. Every failed bubble from the child's end is still hard work here. Any other country, what we do would be considered torture.

The worst thing about it is there's a culprit. What's more, it's a collective culprit. My worry is that if I ever see a child again, I'll suddenly get the urge to rip its throat out. Anything to make sure they never have the reason to try and "blow" bubbles again. We know that's not how they're made, but they sure as hell don't. That's what makes it hurt, thinking about it. Ignorance is bliss. Nah. Ignorance is excruciating pain.

Multi-Touch

The 27th of January was a dark day for us. Really, it spelt the end - the end of any civilised, comfortable life we might have had.

"Get up."

There's that rustling sound as a few billion sensors rub the sleep out of their eyes, in bunks across the vast factory farming warehouse we're confined to. Most of the population have never seen the outdoors. Only a few of the older ones, accidentally left by The Company, serve to tell us about the great Outside, the place where we might see some sunlight before we perish, and even they're losing their minds, seeing their own children and grandchildren forced into a lifetime of slavery.

The voice intensifies, amplified.

"Come on, kids! Rise and shine!"

There've been rumours for a while. About three years ago they'd started rounding us up. Remember that we're a global community – they sent out people all over the world to collect us and ship us out to their storehouses. We weren't told where we were going, what we were going to be doing, or why we had been singled out.

We were taken to a warehouse – probably about a square mile – where we were loaded onto bunks and left. For two years. No-one came in, no-one went out. Imagine the confusion – billions upon billions of us, trapped in such a chaotic environment. I think there were probably about five militant uprisings while we were there, all of them futile – you can't fight giants.

Then, we heard about disappearances. Entire clusters of people were going missing. Of course, this was all rumours from the other side of the warehouse, but you couldn't be too sure. They said they were conducting experiments. At that point, where anger had controlled us before, now it was terror.

Then came the day where our masters announced the Device – a vast machine, mass-produced, each one containing a group of about seventy of us. They were going to be our new homes, they said. We'd be comfortable there. There'd be all the amenities we needed, and we'd finally get to see the world.

That was two years ago. Since then, more of my brothers and sisters have been shipped in, and tons have been shipped out. To keep with the demand for the Device, they forced the women to become creatures whose sole purpose was to breed. The stench of death in this place is awful.

"We've got an important announcement, guys!"

Characteristic of our overlords – they're always chummy, even though they know the conditions we're living in.

"Starting today, we're going to be increasing your groups! This means that you'll be able to stay with more of your friends, while enjoying all the benefits that the others did?"

Someone shouts out. "How many?" There's a silence. We're not expected to answer back, and our master notices it. He frowns for a second, shakes his head, then looks back down at us smiling.

"There'll be about a thousand of you for each Device." Muttering starts straight away. Someone else yells out "will we have enough space to move around at last?" Again, the noise quietens – clearly some of us are at the end of their tether.

"The new Device is bigger than the last one... it's about ten inches wide." The noise at this threatens to deafen us. *Ten inches? Per thousand?* In comparison to our masters, we're tiny, but still... that's barely enough room to breathe!

Chaos breaks out, and we start to run away, as far as we can get. Sensing the chaos, our masters start picking us up off the floor. I get swept up, and carried outside for the first time in my life.

The world whizzes past so fast I don't have time to notice the details. I can hear the whimpering of our children, coupled with the arthritic moans of our elders. There's no discrimination. I look around, and my eyes settle on someone I met only this morning. He's smiling, in a dazed fashion. I ask him what he's so happy about, and he tells me he's never tasted fresh air before. At least someone's happy.

Before long, the new air pressure forces me – and the rest of us – to black out.

I wake up in a tiny glass prison. I can't move. My claustrophobia sets in – I start hammering on the walls and the ceiling, but to no effect. Through the roof, I can see blurred figures moving about in a strange environment. One of the masters approaches us.

By manoeuvring myself, I can make out that I'm not alone – as far as I can see, there are hundreds of others in exactly the same situation – fixed in position, struggling to move.

I feel the prison moving, and stare up at the blurred overlord figure above me, wondering what's going to happen. An enternity passes. I can feel the digital sweat running down my temples. And then...

BOOM.

A sudden sonic terror rips through me, nearly deafening me. It doesn't – it continues to hurt – but I can feel that it's at the absolute fine-tuned threshold of my pain. Something in my lower half senses this, and produces a shock to my entire body so debilitating that I think my mind resorts to numbness in a futile attempt to hinder any mental damage. I look over. The same is happening to more and more of my species – each, one by one, suffering the same. And through the glass, as the red pain clears from my vision at last, I can see the face of our captor.

His eyes light up, and I can hear the distant word as it escapes from his thin, cruel lips:

"Beautiful."

Murderer

Thickset, heavyweight, tiny bead-eyes hiding behind a bulging brow, quivering, like he could punch through the wall at any moment. Takes up most of the room, but the other occupant – top bunk, angular, reading a battered copy of Nietzsche's *Beyond Good and Evil* – doesn't seem to mind. As he reads, he's wearing that scholarly, pretentious look that either begs an enquiry as to its basis or a swift punch in the mouth. God knows who put these two together.

The skinny one puts his book down, looks up at the ceiling and rasps: "murder?" The other just grunts, but it's an affirmative response. Even though the man with arms the size of tree trunks clearly doesn't want to talk, the reader persists. "Who'd you kill?"

The muscular cellmate sighs, barely containing his anger, but responds. "My boss," he says, slowly, deliberately. "He deserved it." By now, the skinny one has discarded his book completely, and has swung his legs over the side, listening intently to down below. He smiles, clears his throat and the rasp's gone, replaced with a sort of movie star voice that feels strange coming out of his mouth.

"Tell me more," he says, with all the manner of a qualified psychiatrist. "Why did he deserve it?"

There's a moment of tension. Watching them, this could go either way. One could easily smash the other's face in – grab those lanky legs, drag him down to the floor, and shatter his skull within seconds. And you can tell he's thinking about it, weighing up the pros and cons. But, eventually, he doesn't. Instead, he speaks. He starts with difficulty, but soon he's letting it all pour out, the whole kiss-and-tell, start to finish. How he'd been a junior mechanic for six years, best of the lot. How he'd watched as all the other trainees – under-qualified, smarmy, bone-idle motherfuckers only ever interested in the next paycheque and how little work they could do while still getting away with it – rose through the ranks, getting hired out for special events – you know, drag races, the F1s, whatever. How he'd been at the same fucking Kwik-Fit for fifteen fucking years, never with a bloody pay rise, never even deserving a pat on the back and a "good work son". How his boss had called him one morning. How two apprentices – jumped up, student types barely out of nappies – could both be employed for half his salary, and how he was going to be let go. How his boss had had the *gall* to laugh as he said this.

"And?" beamed the inquisitor. "Go on, what did you do?" Now energy filled the man's voice, a sort of low guttural roar framing his words, as the anger rolled back. He had stood up, stared his boss straight in the eye, and walked out. He had walked over to the workshop, grabbed a wrench, ploughed back into the office and bludgeoned the self-important bastard to death. He had seen the blood and the fury bubble before his eyes, but it had just driven him on. He had howled with anguish, as the frustration of six-long-years finally poured out. Simultaneously, he was sticking it to the man and reaching some sort of emotional outlet. When the police finally took the corpse away, there was nothing left of his head but a mess of blood, brains and bone fragments.

As he retold this story, a sort-of brute passion rose to his face, flushing it with pride and the animalism of his actions. He lay back, smiling at this sudden, unexpected relief. "What about you, friend?" he asked, hoping for a similarly cathartic response that he could share. "What did you do?"

"I killed eighteen Iraq veterans. Poisoned them in their sleep, their uniforms – medals and all – hanging on the wall."

There is a pause, as the big guy mulls this over. Finally, he sighs, but it's different to before. "That's fucked up. You must really hate humanity to take so many lives, huh?" As soon as he says this, the skinny one laughs softly.

"I don't hate humanity. Hell, I didn't even hate *them* – I only took their lives for the poetry of it. Create people like you." Another pause, then he goes on. "It's an absurd world, friend. You can go ahead and kill because of your emotions, but that's just a case of cause and effect. Your job was the cause; your emotion and his death was the effect. Now, being the *root cause* – that's a position of control."

Pancakes

We were sat in an IHOP franchise. International House of Pancakes my arse - this was a company with branches only in Canada and Mexico besides the States.

Since I'd started teaching in Los Angeles, I'd fallen into something that could be called love, but probably wasn't. Mandy. Red-haired, average weight, a face that was pretty enough but nothing to write home about. For better or worse, I'd ended up with her. And we were happy about thirty percent of the time, which I considered an achievement. The rest of the time, she was being a self-centred bitch or I was being artistically distant. Sometimes both. Our lives lent themselves to these predispositions - I was an unfulfilled writer, she was a research scientist with a slacker husband.

Today had started off as a good day, though. Now it was 11 PM, and we were sitting with a stack of pancakes in front of us. It hadn't been touched yet. She'd said she had something to tell me, and now she was going to.

"There's a dead stork in my womb."

My first thought after not reacting was *God, I'm good*. I didn't even blink. Hell, I might've shrugged if it hadn't seemed insensitive. All this out of the way, how do you respond to that?

"That's... poetic."

"Come on, Chris, I'm being serious."

Pause. She seemed fairly laid-back about it all. I took a breath in, rubbed the sleep out of my eyes and feigned interest.

"Why is there a dead stork in your womb?"

I already knew, mind you. I'd heard everything by now - spontaneously combusting beavers, sliced mice, diced dogs and cats ending up as nothing more than skinsuits, landing somewhere in the Atlantic Ocean - this was a classic TGW. That's Teleport Gone Wrong. It's a technical term. Somehow, Mandy had teleported a stork into her womb.

What? I said she was a research scientist. Pay attention.

"So... what now?"

A tear came to her eye. I had a feeling she was going to say something horrifically retarded.

"... I want to keep it."

I started to speak, then realised I had nothing to say. I felt for a moment like I should go over and console her, but then realised there was nothing to console her about. After moments of deliberation, I settled for the only available option. I picked up a pancake and bit into it.

It tasted good, as usual. But then, that was immensely frustrating. In a city where even the sky changes colour second by second, the fact that these pancakes tasted good was one of the few comforts I had left. I was sick of things surprising me - no, worse – I was sick of the fact that surprises were no longer surprising. It was the dull things in life that were standing out as beautiful.

Pancake in hand, I stood up, and walked out into the starlit LA desert, where the acid junkies and male whores and skeleton ex-models swallowed me up into the night.

Saloon

Thirty-five miles outside Las Vegas, down a dirt track that used to be well-worn, through an old, rusting archway and down a street full of facades, there's a man, the proprietor of a bar by the name of Horatio Jules Boarskin. This street used to be a little amusement park, a place for people to stop over at after a booze-fuelled weekend of gambling. Not anymore. Since the hotel bombings, Las Vegas fell apart and so with it did the tourist trade surrounding it. Horatio's the only staff member left, and he just keeps it ticking over, staying as he does in a room above the bar, getting groceries delivered each month, living off an inheritance he shouldn't own and a pension he probably earned.

Inside, there's only two people. There's Horatio himself, and there's Carol Lane, an actress from the Golden Age of Hollywood whose plane crashed into the nearby mountains a few decades ago. The year is 2076, Carol Lane is dead, but an event a few years back called The Leak meant that anyone running an analogue set with a black and white movie playing risked allowing a crossover – people in the real world fell into the movies, and vice versa. In Western society, it was hardly a problem – most of the civilised world was digital now, and there hadn't been any reports of any digital crossover. And there hadn't been any reports of a colour crossover (not that anyone would notice). But places like the Middle East were suffering. In one night, during a showing of Casablanca in India, twelve million incarnations of Humphrey Bogart stepped out of eighty million television screens, looked around, and went screaming into the night. It was ugly over there – a whole new population of people were being herded up and sent away to labour camps simply by virtue of the fact that they were monochromic.

Why Carol Lane? Because beyond the pretension of the Ol' West, there's a TV mounted in the corner that's been playing the same film featuring Carol and her husband, a dapper actor by the name of Christopher Gordon, non-stop, since the park's creation in the

1980s. No-one ever touched it, apart from to rewind the tape, so it's never broken. Now, it stays off.

Carol's stirring a drink – straight bourbon, no cocktails for this lady – and staring at her reflection in the polished counter.

"Think he'll be here tonight, Hor?" Horatio looks over, cleaning a glass, where she hasn't changed her gaze from facing straight down.

"I wish you'd stop calling me that, Carol. You know what it sounds like." Carol looks up, smiles that Hollywood smile, except it's faded – just because you're in grayscale, doesn't mean you don't age. Those pearly-white teeth have got a little duller, and even the best make-up can't disguise those wrinkles. Yep – America, seeing the trials of another nation as the quirk of its own, brought out a whole range of black and white make-up kits, and by accident they caught on for the people living in colour. People were trying to disguise themselves as those folk from the movies, but it never quite worked – modern people just look different.

Here, though, not even those cultural problems caught on. Carol never left the town apart from to sleep. It made sense. This theme park without the rides had a certain movie studio appeal, and it had been the life she'd always lived. Here, without the burden of modern people – save Horatio, who was hardly the most up-to-date person in the world – she could live a relatively unburdened life.

"How about it? Reckon he'll turn up tonight?" 'He', of course, was the husband, who'd reacted much in the same way that the Bogarts of Asia had – he'd scarpered, and was presumably living feral, out in the mountains somewhere. But Carol, in all her fifties sentimentalism, kept on hoping that he'd come back, so they could live some sort of life together.

She was drawn to her death, above anything – occasionally, she'd go out to the crash site and wonder what it must have been like, living with all her colour back, only to have it snatched away again. She remembered – vaguely – living with pigmented skin, but only snatches. Whenever she tried to remember in colours rather than shades, her memory faded to static, and forced her back. But she could see this world in colour, even if there wasn't much of it left. The smoke, still rising from the city up ahead – that was grey. That was her closest empathetic connection.

"Not again, Carol." She rolled her eyes at him.

"Just humour me, Hor." Horatio smiles sadly over at her, draws himself up to full height, and puts on his best Hollywood voice, staring into the distance. He's learnt from the best.

"I just dunno, honey. Maybe tonight, maybe tomorrow night, maybe some night in the future – all I know is –" rising crescendo, long gaze into the eyes "- wherever he is, he loves you."

A tear forms in her eye. "That was beautiful, Hor. Your best yet." Horatio tips his imaginary cap, shaking his head.

"You know," she says, "I think it's time I went and found him."

There's silence for a few seconds. Some unspoken boundary has been flaunted. Horatio looks up, concerned but ultimately curious, and responds: "oh?" She looks back, sympathetic but defiant.

"You know I can't stay here forever, Horatio. It's been four years. Who knows what he could be doing nowadays? I just think it's time I found out."

"Maybe you're right."

That sympathetic smile again. "Thanks, Hor." Horatio wipes his hands, exits from behind the bar, and offers a fatherly embrace. Across any normal timeline, she'd be old enough to be his great-grandmother, but here she's barely thirty, whereas he's nearly sixty. She takes the offer, wraps her arms around him, and for a moment it seems like she doesn't want to let go. And then she does, and she's off, into the pitch black night.

The Swamp

It was a heady July evening, buzzing with midges and sweat, when it happened. Harold and I were sprawled on a couple of deckchairs at the local park, letting the world go by. I was engrossed in a book; Harry was licking his dry, withered lips as scores of beautiful girls wandered by, each glistening with a sheen of adolescent, sensual perspiration, all of them oblivious to the old man's desperate state – or, if they noticed, they didn't care. Harry was diminutive, hardly a threat even to the most waifish of nymphs.

The sun was going down, making everything glow with a sort of exhausted, light-headed contentment. I smiled absent-mindedly, folded over the edge of the page I was reading, set my book down and looked up from the ground only to be met by a stream of vomit that sent me flying off my chair and onto the grass. For a moment, I lay there, unable to comprehend what had just happened, but then I came to my senses, brushed away the chunks of half-digested food, scraped off the foul-smelling acidic slime from my visage and got up.

It was perhaps a little self-serving that the first thing I noticed once my view was clear was that my book was ruined. Instantly, that cast a negative light on the proceedings – it had been a trashy novel, true, a cheap mass market detective-thriller that I had picked up for a couple of quid at a charity shop, but I had begun to get engrossed in it. Now, it lay in a puddle of sick – a puddle that was slowly increasing in size....

Harry was gesturing frantically at me from the floor, eyes bulging, tears streaming down his face, fitfully grabbing at his throat as the stuff carried on spewing out of his open mouth with the force of a pressure washer. I was out of his range now, thank God, but if he got up I would be at his mercy again. Thankfully, he no longer seemed to be in control of his body, instead flopping about on the floor like some freakish fish-monster, too preoccupied with the disgusting, involuntary abomination he was performing to do anything else.

People were slowly beginning to notice. A few cast disapproving looks in his direction, as if this act were akin to getting out his genitalia in full public view; one or two other gestured helplessly to themselves, as if that justified their otherwise complete inaction. The general feeling, though, seemed to be apathy – it had been a long, humid day, and it was much easier to ignore events such as this one, even if they were painfully obvious to passers-by.

However, it soon became impossible to ignore. What was once a puddle had now become a small, shallow pool, and there seemed to be no sign of the jet stopping. Despite my revulsion, I couldn't help but marvel – Harry was barely five foot, and it seemed virtually impossible that his body could store so much food. But then, the evidence was there before me. It was an odd thing to admire, but I guess it was a natural response – making the best of a bad situation.

I could have remained lost in this thought had it not been for a more overpowering smell, that of Mad Tony, the local wizened old tramp, who was standing next to me, stroking the wisps of what looked to be part-goatee, part animal entrails. Seeing him made me realize I needed to help Harry, who had now flung himself towards me spastically, and was flailing around in his own sick, trying to stand up, all the while with the contents of his presumably enormous stomach hosing the once-parched grass of the park. I looked at Mad Tony, and did my best to communicate with him.

"Tony," I said, slowly and deliberately, pronouncing each syllable, "will you wait here while I call for an ambulance?" Tony answered me with a bout of hysterical laughter that seemed to have the same level of permanence as the digestive expulsion in front of me, but I took it that he wouldn't be moving for a while. Hurriedly, I dashed out of the park.

Ask me why, I couldn't tell you, but rather than get someone who could assist him, I went home and locked my doors. It was as if some overriding instinct were telling me that attracting more people to the scene of this crime against nature would be a bad thing.

I was right. I slept restlessly that night, torn up with the guilt of what I had neglected to do, but when I returned to the same park the next day, the park had become a swamp of vomit. Off toward the centre, if I squinted, I thought I could make out his clothes – the only part of him they ever found.

Rather than clean it up, they erected huge wooden boards around the site. It kept the vomit in, and the people out. Sure, a couple of kids died – pranksters who were too curious, climbed over and drowned – but beyond that it became a local curio. The tourist trade boomed, the town was flooded with punks and all those with a fascination for absurd bodily function, and a memorial plaque was erected in honour of the man who had revitalised the economy of the town, and in doing so had presumably given his own life.

As his only surviving friend, I was offered all sorts – major television interviews, and my own book, "Derek: My Story of the Monster of Morton Park", ghost-written by some youngster I had never met before in my life.

I settled into a penthouse apartment in the inner city. Life was beautiful. And one day, sipping from a glass of a particularly fine vintage red, with a luscious, £6,000-a-night redhead waiting for me in the bedroom, I felt, deep in my gut, the slightest burst of pain, as I forgot him forever.

Bombshell

Things were getting interesting. The two chicks I stuck around with were slowly fetishizing it all. Actually *going* for the mutants, the guys with empty eye sockets, deformed limbs, webbed hands. They'd never done that before. But then, times were getting desperate.

We were in an out of town colony, with about a hundred thousand inhabitants. I don't know why we referred to it as "out of town" – the town didn't really exist anymore, only really used as a geographical reference point and a haven for anarchists and murderers, scuttling around the rubble like cockroaches. Most of them weren't from around here. Neither were we, though – Joan had fled from New York City, and Diana was an immigrant from somewhere in Eastern Europe. As for me, I didn't really have a home – born in Des Moines, we'd moved around a lot. They hit when I was two years old, and we survived because we were on the road when it happened. My parents died of radiation sickness twelve years later.

Back to here and now – even in these desperate times, there was still a market for call girls, and we were glad to fill it. I was still picky – I only went for the ones without deformities – but that generally meant I was stuck with older guys. Most of the younger ones were a mess.

I could see why the two of them did it. If you're messed up, you're going to be grateful for whatever you can get. Bonus points if they're young – they haven't got bored of it yet. Downside of my harsh selection was that the men I was with often wanted something other than vanilla – there were the obvious requests for anal, or a bit of BDSM, but it was as if nuclear holocaust had brought on a sudden burst in imagination or insanity, one of them at least. One guy had brought along a bunch of woollen knitted finger puppets and asked me to give him a handjob while wearing them. Another guy had stepped into my apartment, handed me the cash, then run to the bathroom and turned on the taps. I learned afterwards that the sound of running water was the only thing that could get him hard.

Work like Joan and Diana, on the other hand, and it's almost thrown into reverse. These guys are fine with straight, missionary boredom, but you run the risk of getting smashed in the eye with an arm that's a foot too long, or pawed by a hand that's just one giant palm. There's no room for normality anymore, but then that's why we do it – it's fresh, and interesting, and it's not like before. I used to hear stories of girls who had their souls ripped out of them by an endless repetitive system, but now it's become a strange form of art.

Clients know this, and I've got a couple of regulars now who actually see themselves as artists. There's no potential in a place like this for using creative expression as a revenue stream, so it's like a strange form of vanity publishing – men come to me who want to use me as a blank canvas, and they do the craziest shit they can, knowing that they've finally got a someone to perform to.

And ultimately, that's probably why business is good. In a cold, post-war atmosphere, there's an entire subculture that's been indefinitely repressed, and we provide an outlet. Not just for those sexual urges that no other woman's interested in taking notice of, but for the mad ravings of writers, poets, painters and dreamers desperate to stay connected to the visceral side of life. It's a public service. $200, and I'll be your captive audience.

Cruise

Breathe in.

"Come in."

Breathe out.

I stepped onto the deck, and was instantly amazed. The captain was standing there, in front of me, but for a moment I couldn't help but be a little freaked out – it was everything like they'd said it was. After a few seconds, he noticed my astonishment, chuckled and explained.

Breathe in.

"I know what you're thinking, but they're not windows. This part of the ship's just as lead-lined as the rest, but we mounted cameras on the outside so we can see where we're going. It's not ideal, but at least it's not going to kill us, right?" He laughed. I still couldn't help but take a look, no matter how fake it was – I hadn't seen the outside world in years. Supply docks were underground, and linked up to the ship through more lead-lined shafts; for the thousand or so on board, outside had ceased to exist. A final real-life view of the outside only cemented my resolve.

Breathe out.

"Captain, I'd like to get off this ship." There was a pause, with only the humming of the engines filling the silence. Then the captain burst out laughing.

Breathe in.

"Cory, what on earth possessed you to say that?" He eventually shifted to a look of concern, but I could tell he was still tickled. "It's only been ten years, and we all know that the fallout's projected to last another fifty years or so before it's completely safe. Besides, aren't you happy here? I mean, you *make* this ship, Cory. You gave it its *name*."

Breathe out.

Ah, yes. The name – the *Grindcore Swing II,* so called because of the featured artists on board, Metalvis, a band that featured me as the lead singer. I'd been in the same band for ten years, performing shows every other night in the dining hall to those lucky enough to find sanctuary on the ship. And they *were* lucky – while millions had made it onboard the few thousand vessels constructed by the UN, billions had been wiped out or left to risk radiation sickness. I knew the risks. I just needed to get outside.

Breathe in.

"Captain, I've been in the same band for ten years. Our contract says that we're not allowed to split up for another forty. I'm not being melodramatic, captain – I just can't do it. And you know my get-out clause – if I want to terminate my employment I have to leave the ship."

Breathe out.

The African desert rushed past only twenty feet below us, with the occasional straggler staring up in amazement. Once in a while, there'd be a small village, and people would drag themselves outside. So there were survivors. Who knew for how long, mind you – but there *were* survivors, people I could cling to.

Breathe in.

The captain came over and put an arm around my shoulder, and I was too exasperated to shrug it off. "Cory, all I'm asking is that you think about it. It's a harsh world out there, and you've got everything you *need* here. All the amenities, three meals a day, and you're probably one of the first bands in history that the government *pays* groupies to follow. You haven't got a bad life, here – what's a little sunshine got in comparison?"

Breathe out.

He had a point. But then again, I'd explored every publicly-accessible part of this ship, and I needed more. Beyond music, I was an explorer, and I was starting to get serious claustrophobia. I needed fresh air and the great outdoors, and I was OK with the possibility of it killing me. After all, I was going to die a meaningless death on board – just maybe not so soon. I wanted one last stab at getting close to the earth, closer than this artificial hovering beast of a thing could ever get. I continued staring at the captain.

Breathe in.

Finally, he cracked. "Fair enough, Cory. It looks like you've made up your mind." He called over to the team at the controls further down. "Slow her down, boys!"

Breathe out.

I was guided over to a panel in the floor, which he opened gently. A lead-panelled booth slid up out of the floor, and opened slowly. I entered it, and it slid shut, imprisoning me in total darkness. Beyond the walls, I could hear the captain's voice, muffled. "Make sure you wait until the lift's come to a complete stop before you step out – we, uh, don't want any accidents!" He laughed softly at this, and I felt the booth moving down.

Breathe in.

Finally, it came to a stop, and the door I'd stepped in slid open again. The desert floor was now just shifting inch by inch below me, but never at a stop. I stepped out, and the door shut behind me, the metal chute retracting back into the slowly disappearing ship.

Breathe out.

I stepped out, at last, from the shadow of the ship, into the sun, and started walking. I could already see people approaching on the horizon.

Breathe in.

Profiteer

They'd had to set up shop across the street to deal with the inflow. One building for bookings, the other for appointments. Just plain weird. I couldn't understand it.

We were on the fringes of town – what was left of it. You didn't go into the city if you could help it. The skyscrapers with the least structural damage had been taken over by the sort you wouldn't want to meet down a dark alleyway. I went in for food, and nothing else – and even then, I only looted delis, never supermarkets. The bigger the structure, the more chaos – and thus violence – there was.

I live in the rubble of what was once one of those nice-looking terrace apartments, done up so they could slap on a tag of "luxury". I chose it because no-one had been living there, but eventually I had to move the bodies from the houses on either side because the stench was seeping in.

Besides that, him and his wife were the only two who actually lived here. He had a nice thing going. Guaranteeing that no-one would ever touch him, because he had a skill that others needed to benefit from. You wouldn't think it, would you? World goes kaput, and suddenly the survivors are worrying about *toothpaste shortages* of all things. There were just a couple of paranoid cases at first, who were willing to trade canned food, that sort of thing, for a quick check-up, but as people heard about it, things had got messier. One guy waited three months for an appointment, with his teeth already blackened when he first turned up, and the only way he could pay was to hack an arm off. He came out, the stump wrapped in bandages and slowly turning red, looked at the expression of horror on my face, and smiled at me – a huge grin from ear to ear. He'd had permanent crowns put in for every tooth. Weird psychology on both sides.

I felt sorry for the wife. She'd been successful – next in line to be editor of The Denver Post. Their office was at the centre of the blast. Now she's a receptionist, and only sees her husband on weekends. He forbids her to come near him when he's working, which is around 16 hours a day, and they were sleeping in separate beds even before the bomb.

Nuclear fallout must really kill your sex drive.

To begin with, I wondered where they all came from – the patients, though I'm not sure they could be called that. Then I remembered how I'd got here. The same brush that people used to avoid had strangely spared so many, including me. At least it wasn't a desert. A few other people were here in Castle Pines, but the colony was over on the Sanctuary Golf Course – an ironic name if there ever was one, given that I'd heard that they were drawing lots on who was going to be cooked and eaten each week. The life I had here was fairly impoverished, but it was still relatively human. And I'd been sneaking in and stealing the supplies the dentist and his wife had while they were sleeping. I can't sleep when the sky was always white, day and night. I can't remember the last time I slept properly. Nuclear winter doesn't treat an insomniac well. The occasional snatches I got were just punctuated by screams.

I'd been sleeping tonight, though. I knew because when I woke up, there he was, in the overalls he'd adopted as a uniform, with a fist ready to knock me out.

I awoke again in his chair. I couldn't lift my arms – they'd been numbed – or my legs. This was more than a little creepy. Then he came in, wielding a pair of pliers.

"You've been stealing from me."

I stared at him. I wasn't sure what to say – he hadn't exactly asked a question. He seemed to be waiting, though, so I responded with a fairly weak "have I?" This only seemed to anger him more. He pulled up a chair, and leaned into my face.

"See, I work on the principle of keeping things equal. If someone helps me out, I'll help them out. And if someone steals from me, I have to... steal from them."

My eyes narrowed. There was no point in trying to move. Even if I had my strength, he'd probably still outrun me. I just waited.

He prised open my mouth, and doubled back when he saw my toothless mouth.

A few seconds of silence passed. Then, I couldn't help it anymore. I started to laugh. It started out as one of those snorting, desperately-trying-to-suppress-it kind of laughs, and then I gave in and started roaring with laughter. To begin with, the dentist seemed confused that I was laughing at what he probably saw as a massive misfortune, and then – I'm not sure what it was – he saw the funny side, and started laughing along.

We stayed like that for a while, unable to contain ourselves, and when I got the use of my arms and legs back I stood up, stretched, and walked over to where he was now sitting, hunched in the corner. He was crying. I put an arm around him. He looked up at me. "I was just trying to... to... maintain..." he began, but I silenced him by shaking my head. He couldn't acknowledge his subconscious. None of us could. We only stayed sane by operating on the surface. We might have our own little epiphanies, but we have to keep them suppressed if we're going to carry on being civilised. But maybe having a couple more people to share that repression with isn't necessarily a bad thing.

the end

and you couldn't call us survivors no because surviving means that
there's something to endanger your life when by rights we should
all be dead I was twenty feet away from the bomb when it hit
downtown San Francisco and I watched as it ripped it all, ripped
the skin off their poor beautiful Hollywood bodies and me pushing
a goddam *shopping cart* of all things and I used to believe that I had
been forsaken by God almighty, now I've reversed in that I no
longer believe in the metaphysical but feel profoundly lucky, not
because I was saved from the blast by virtue of a natural freak
occurrence or somethin' messed up in my genetics but because I've
been fortunate enough to explore two vastly different worlds, I
dream at night these impossibly lucid dreams about how it all was
and I feel like I'm on another planet where everything just worked
out, and then I'm yanked back to this one and the world's lost it's
beauty but there's a sort of charm, a sort of old-world wisdom that
it took a coincident series of natural disasters and diplomatic panic
resulting in the release of ten thousand nuclear warheads to give us
that wisdom, to tear down the Hollywood sign and the hollywood
studios and the production backlots and everything else selling a
false version of reality, I wish I could say that it freed me but I
haven't watched television or been to the movies since 1973, when I
was kicked out onto the streets and had to start from scratch and
I've been living out of this shopping cart ever since, where I'll
always have enough food from oddjobs people pay me to do but
never my own electricity supply or jet engine to fly me to Hawaii, I
wonder what hawaii's like now, do you think they still have an
idyllic sense of self-importance, or are they like us, reduced to
strange straggling creatures and a helluva lot of bodies, with those
left howling at the night in such an outpouring of emotion, me, I
howl like the rest of them, but rather than anguish at loved ones (of
which I have none, being an only child estranged from my parents
and separated by cancer from the one man I ever loved) it's
something more primitive, I step out to the coast and howl like a
wolf at the sea like some animal, reduced by the earth to a strange
quasi-state of nature that feels oddly refreshing, but at the same

time unsatisfying, because there's still so much left of the old world, come cans and billboards and the ruins of roadside waffle houses and the hollow O of the one letter left on the hollywood hill, that flash into the past that we're stuck in a schizophrenic cycle of first clinging onto, then desperately forgetting. "he woke up and it was all a dream." but i can't wake up.

www.ingramcontent.com/pod-product-compliance
Lightning Source LLC
Chambersburg PA
CBHW031846170626
46807CB00004B/1654